The Giant

The Adventures of Silver Dove, Book Seven

Eliza Scalia

Cover Illustration by: Wayne F. Shurtz and
Cheyanne and Jean Buffkin
Based upon the characters originally
designed by Suji Gallianetti

ISBN-13: 978-1-0881-8698-5

Dedicated to all the people who patiently let me talk endlessly about my stories. Thanks to all of you I was able to think through different ideas and come out with the finished products I have today.

Chapter One
Colomba-
Another Day
Begins

The hallway is filled with noise as I make my way to my next class. Everyone is chatting and laughing, as if they are completely carefree right now. I can understand why they would feel that way, I kind of feel that way too. The Crow hasn't attacked the school in a while and I'm definitely enjoying the break. It has given me a chance to relax and spend some time with my friends. I've really needed this, facing the Crow all the time is really stressful. I swear if he keeps this up, I'm going to have wrinkles by the time I'm twenty.

The last time the Crow tried to do anything, he turned Alex into this creepy bull- man creature thing. It was really weird. It got even weirder though when Alex changed back into his normal self and he told me what the Crow had said to him in his mind. Alex said that the Crow wanted to transform him into a monster so that he can show me just how much of a monster Alex truly is. From what I can tell from that, the Crow seems to have a crush on me or something. This has given me a question that has been running through my head since that happened. Which is worse, having a crazy person like the Crow be your enemy, or having them be in love with you? I don't know what everyone else would say to that, but I think that it would be worse to have them love you. If they just hate you, you know what to expect. The crazy person just wants to hurt you. If the crazy person loves you though, what should you expect? I have no idea what the answer to that question would be, and I don't know if I want to find out or not. Sadly, for me, I have to deal with him being my enemy and being in love with me. He hates me as Silver Dove, but apparently he loves me as myself... Why can't I have normal problems? I mean I have a super villain that wants to hurt me as well as date me, this is not a situation I want to be in. Why couldn't I have had a villain a little less confusing as the Crow? Just a little bit, I would be happy with that.

My thoughts are interrupted as I hear someone shout, "Look out!" I quickly dodge out of the way as a football flies through the air and nearly hits me in the face. I'm not surprised when I look over to see that the ball was thrown by one of Alex's friends from the football team and he was trying to throw it to Alex who picks up the ball and walks over to me with his usual confident grin.

"That was a pretty sweet dodge you just did. Did you just start doing some kind of sport or something recently 'cus your reflexes are fantastic?" I take a deep breath to make sure that I don't yell at him.

"Alex, I've told you a million times that I do martial arts." He nods and smiles at me.

"Oh right, of course. I completely forgot." I turn and walk away from him. A cold, mean little thought runs through my mind. You didn't forget, you just didn't bother to remember. Alex always does stuff like this. He never bothers to listen to anything I say, yet he talks to me almost constantly and expects me to listen to all of it. It is so unfair, but that word can sum up being friends with Alex in general, unfair.

"Hey, are you doing anything after school today?" Alex asks me this with a sly look on his face and I just know that if I tell him that I'm not doing anything then he's going to ask me out. I quickly think of a small lie.

"Yes, I'm super busy tonight. I'm going to be hanging out with Luis and Nat." I notice that Alex's eyes darken when I say that I'm going to be with Luis. I know that he thinks of Luis as competition for my attention and it is driving me nuts. Alex acts as if we are already dating and he's my jealous boyfriend. It's super annoying, just one more confusing problem for me to deal with. Men cause so many problems in my life. He quickly makes that dark expression disappear to be replaced by his usual confident grin.

"Alright, no problem. We can just hang out another day. I'll see you later." He walks off with his usual swagger, but I know that it is just an act. I now know something about Alex that I don't think anybody else at this school does. His dad treats him terribly at home. I found this out after a football game not too long ago. Our school's team had lost and Alex's dad blamed him for that as if it was his fault and then made him walk several miles home in the middle of the night after playing what I'm guessing was a very exhausting game. I'm also guessing that what his dad did was something pretty normal for Alex. I think that his dad does stuff like this all the time. I can't believe that I'm saying this, but I actually feel pretty bad for Alex. I had been trying to avoid him before I saw what happened with his dad, but I'm trying to give him a second chance to be friends with me. I can only hope that he doesn't just end up being a jerk to Luis again. I have my doubts though that he can do something as simple as that.

I turn away from him to head to my next class, hoping that everything will be alright. As I walk alone, I hear a few girls beside me talking loudly and what they're talking about really catches my attention.

"Did you see what Angela put on A- Streamer about Marcia?" The girl that spoke holds up her phone to show her friend. She's obviously got A-Streamer, a social media website that's popular in my town, pulled up on her phone and is showing her friend a post that Angela wrote. The friend glances at the post for only a second before she starts laughing.

"That is so true, Marcia is a complete freak. It's no wonder she's single. Who would want to date someone like her?" The friend continues to laugh as they both walk past me. I watch them as they keep walking.

After everything that has happened with the Crow transforming bullied kids in my school, these girls are still teasing people online? Haven't they learned their lesson? Don't they want the Crow to go away? I don't understand this. Is it just built into some people that they have to bully someone else and beat them down? Why are they doing this when they know it is bad and that some maniac is trying to force people to stop doing this? Why are people so dumb?

Someone else near me must have heard what the girls just said because they say something in response to one of their friends in an angry whisper.

"Did you hear that? The Crow would definitely make them pay for something like that. We should tell everyone at the meeting tonight about this. Maybe one day we can contact the Crow so that he can take care of all this." My heart sinks into my chest. I know what they are talking about. The meeting they are going to has to be for the Crow's fan club. The school didn't let the students form an official club for that, so the students made the club themselves. They meet at a diner in town so the school can't get them in trouble. The club is made up of a bunch of the people who get bullied in this school. It's not a secret that they hate me as Silver Dove too. They would be so happy if the Crow just destroyed me one of these days. They view me as the enemy and him as the hero. Can't they see that I'm just trying to make sure that nobody gets hurt and that people are happy? That's all I want. Why can't things just be simple? Why does everyone have to be out to get me?

I slowly walk down the hall to get to class, but it feels as if I am walking through a sea of people who want nothing more than to hurt me. I feel so alone.

Chapter Two
Luis-
Watching and
Waiting

As the crowd wanders around me, I watch as a girl runs into the bathroom with tears in her eyes while two other girls laugh at her. I know what this is about. Apparently, Angela said something cruel about that girl on A- Streamer last night and now everybody is making fun of her. I bet that a lot of the people teasing her don't even know her. They just like having somebody new to hurt.

After everything I have done as the Crow, have they really not learned anything about how to treat each other? Are they really so stupid that they haven't figured out that if they want me to stop doing what I'm doing as the Crow then they just need to treat each other with some kindness? Considering what I just saw, I must be surrounded by idiots. While I keep walking to my next class, I see the head idiot of this school up ahead of me. Alex is walking down the hall, eagerly trying to walk side by side with Colomba. He almost looks like a needy little puppy chasing after her. He looks so pathetic that I can't help but smile. She's trying very hard to walk quickly away from him, yet he is keeping up with her. My smile gets even bigger when a certain thought crosses my mind. He has to chase after her to be near her, but she is always happy to be around me. Colomba's eyes are clouded with annoyance as he talks to her. Can't that idiot realize that she doesn't want to talk to him? Why does he keep trying? More importantly though, why doesn't Colomba just tell him to back off?

Not too long ago she did that to him, but for some reason she has started talking to him again recently. I have an idea as to why that may have happened. A few weeks ago, I transformed Alex into a monster right before a big football game. Silver Dove came, of course, and defeated him, and the game went on as it was supposed to. The game wasn't too important to me, what really matters is what happened afterward. After the game I saw Alex talking to his dad, and his dad treated him like he was a disgusting bug beneath his foot. He treated Alex as if he was an enemy, not his only son. I actually felt pity for him for a little bit. Only for a little bit though. I won't let what I saw affect how I feel about him or change my plans. Just because someone is cruel to him doesn't mean that he can be cruel to others. I think that Colomba may have seen what happened too. She must have felt the same pity that I had so she let him start talking with her again. I think she's regretting that decision now though, judging from how annoyed she looks while Alex walks beside her, showing off about how he and his family will be going out on their boat this weekend. He is kind of implying that he wants her to come with him, but Colomba is ignoring him. She obviously doesn't care even though I know that a lot of girls would love to be in her shoes. I've heard countless girls talk about how cute they think Alex is and how they have the biggest crushes on him. Every time I hear that I think I'm going to get sick. How anybody could have a crush on a cruel idiot like him, I will never know.

My thoughts are interrupted when someone runs up from behind me and rams their shoulder into mine, knocking some books out of my hands. The guy laughs wickedly before running off down the hall while I stoop down to pick them up. I don't even bother to feel hurt anymore, I've become too used to this kind of stuff to really feel anything anymore. Sometimes it's hard to feel anything at all.

Chapter Three
Colomba-
Whispered Words

I step into my classroom, finally getting rid of Alex. I told myself, after how I saw his dad treat him, that I would be friendlier to Alex again. He is making that very difficult though. Alex can be so annoying. He's always following me around and showing off. I don't know how long I can be nice to him if he keeps going on like this. I know that a lot of girls would find him charming if he was talking to them the way he's been talking to me, but I see him as he is, just a flirt.

I sit at my desk and bury my face in my hands. I sigh softly, trying to get rid of some of my annoyance before class starts. This doesn't work though since I overhear something that makes me even more annoyed.

"Did you hear what Angela said about Tania?" I glance over to my side to see two girls standing close to each other, as if they don't want anybody to overhear them even though they are talking pretty loudly.

"No, what?" The girl's friend asks curiously.

"Angela said that she went to Alex Donner's party this weekend and started throwing up in the pool." The friend's eyes open wide in shock as they start laughing.

"You're kidding me!" The girl who is spreading this little rumor just smiles, knowing that she has her friend's full attention.

"Nope, Angela says that she saw it with her own eyes."

"How did I not hear about this before?" The girl spreading the rumor leans in even closer, but she is still talking loud enough for me to hear her.

"Well apparently it happened at the end of the party when practically everyone had gone home. Angela was one of the last people there and she was the only one who saw it all happen." I turn away from them, trying not to scream. How stupid are these girls? Why are they believing anything that Angela was saying? Angela is well known in this school for being a snobby mean girl, as well as a huge liar. Why should they believe something she said when nobody else seems to have seen it? This is probably just a lie like usual, but these girls, for some reason, believe it. What is wrong with them? Do they just want to have someone to pick on?

I know the party they are talking about. Alex tried to invite me to it, but I declined. I know what that party would have been like if I did go. There would have been loud music playing to entertain a massive group of people crowded into one house, everyone having to bump into each other just to move from one place to another. You would have to scream just to be heard over the loud music and other people talking. The party would be filled with people I don't hang out with, probably just people from the sports teams that Alex is a part of, as well as some girls that aren't the type I usually hang out with. Somebody would always be doing something stupid and there was always a chance somebody would call the cops because of the noise. Also, I know that if I went to Alex's party, he would be hanging around me the entire time, trying to show me off to his friends. That does not sound like a good time to me, so I declined the offer. I do know this though, if somebody did throw up in Alex's pool, he would have told everyone about it, and he would have definitely told me about it since he tells me about everything else going on in his life. What Angela said is a lie, and they are spreading terrible rumors about a girl who didn't even do anything wrong.

I want to scream at these girls and give them a piece of my mind, but I know that it would be pointless, I hear stuff like this all the time. If I told off these girls it wouldn't stop stuff like this from happening, I would just be embarrassing myself. I used to not notice the rumors spreading or the people getting picked on very often. That is, I didn't notice until the Crow showed up. When I first saw him and he was blathering on about helping all the bullied kids, that's when I started paying attention so that I could help these people before the Crow noticed them too and would try to "help" them. Before that, it's not like I didn't care, it's just that it was kind of invisible to me. My grandma tells me that I'm a bit naïve at times and that I don't see or understand some things. I'm a very smart person, I know that, but my grandma says that I just see the world as a more peaceful and kind place than it actually is. I would like to think that I am just a happy person who likes to see the good in the world, but I know that my grandma is right. I used to ignore the darkness around me, but thanks to the Crow, I can't hide from it anymore. I can't hide and I don't know what to do sometimes. It feels as if I am an alien who has just left their home planet and is now exploring a completely new planet that I know nothing about. It is not a fun feeling.

As the girls continue their gossiping, I pick up a book to read so that I can ignore them. This is not easy though. When I try to focus on the story in my book, their voices just seem to get louder and louder, their words getting more and more cruel. I don't know this Tania girl that they are talking about, but my heart aches for her and I can only hope that she will never have to hear the mean words that I am hearing about her now.

Chapter Four
Luis-
Cruel and Kind
Words

Walking down the hallway in school is always an adventure, but not the fun kind of adventure. Every time I walk through the halls alone it is a guessing game of whether or not I'm going to get hurt by one of the many people who like to pick on me. Everyone is chatting to their friends, laughing loudly, and just causing chaos. The noise in the hall is so loud that a pounding starts in my head. I close my eyes and take in a deep breath, trying to make my head feel better. Someone notices this since they take advantage of my moment of weakness.

My eyes open wide in shock as a cold liquid is poured down my back. I let out a small shout of surprise that makes several people around me laugh. My eyes dart around the hall, trying to find out who did this to me. It isn't very hard for me to find out who that person is. Some guy I don't even know is standing near me with an empty water bottle in his hand. I want to be mad at him, but all I can think is how lucky I am. A lot of the times when people do stuff like this to me, it's soda or something worse. Having water poured down my back isn't as bad; it isn't sticky like soda when it dries and it's not something gross like I've had many times before. I smile softly at the guy and he stops laughing to look at me with surprise. I enjoy his confusion for a moment before walking away. They all laugh at me, thinking that I am defeated, but they would all be surprised if they knew who they just messed with. If they knew, they would beg for mercy. The only problem would be trying to figure out whether or not I should give them that mercy. If they do stuff like this to me all the time and they don't even know me, then do they really deserve mercy? I smile at that thought as I continue to walk down the hallway.

Even though so many people laughed at my pain, two people apparently don't find it amusing. I feel a hand rest on my shoulder, and I look to my side to see two students that I sort of recognize from middle school. They are losers just like me. One is a guy named Omar who is an outcast due to the fact that he is from a foreign country and everyone thinks that his accent sounds hilarious. The person with him is a girl named Anna, but she prefers to be called Moon. She can easily be described as a goth girl; she always wears black and has black lipstick that really sticks out since she is so pale.

"We saw what happened back there, we are sorry that they did that." Omar says with complete honesty.

"Yeah, don't worry about it though, the Crow

will fix all of them sooner or later." Moon says with a cold sneer on her face. "Once he finally makes his final move, we won't have to worry about people like that guy messing with us." Omar nods at her words with approval.

"Yes, once he comes back, things will be better for everyone. Let's just hope that day will come soon. I've seen people messing with you many times, you should come and join the Crow's Club, we would love to have you." I smile at the mention of my group of supporters, my fan club. It's nice to know that they still support me even though I haven't really won against Silver Dove yet. I tell them that I can't, that my uncle heard about the club and said that if I join them then I will be punished. The two seem to understand and they say goodbye before they walk down the hall together.

I almost want to laugh about how ironic that was. It's crazy to think that they were comforting their hero and praising me without knowing who I really am. I wonder how they would act if they knew who I really am. I have a pretty good guess as to what they would do, they would probably freak out and beg to help me. I'm kind of tempted to do that now, but I know I can't. I need to fight this battle myself.

Of course, what I told them was a complete lie. My uncle doesn't know about the club as far as I know, but if I join them then I might accidently reveal something and they will know who I am. Even though that thought is tempting, I can't drag anybody else into my war with Silver Dove and this school. This is my fight, and I don't want anybody to get hurt.

Before I walk into my next class, I look back at the figures of Omar and Moon down the hall. As I watch someone make rude remarks to Omar, I can only hope that I won't disappoint them in the end. I can only feel surprised that I have any fans left by this point. I have failed so many times that I almost feel like giving up sometimes. I once heard that a way to describe insanity is that a person does something over and over again and expects a different result. Maybe that's what I am doing. I am constantly trying to come back as the Crow, giving somebody superpowers, and then having that person getting beaten by Silver Dove. Even though I have lost, I still try again, and I still expect to win the next time. Maybe I am insane for thinking that I will beat her one day. Maybe I should just give up and join Silver Dove's side like she is always telling me I should do. Maybe then I can have some peace in my life.

As I continue watching Omar and Moon walking down the hallway with people throwing insults at them, I know that I can't give up. I have to keep fighting for them. I need to fight for the people who can't fight for themselves. I need to help the weaker people. I was once one of those weak people. I know how it feels to feel powerless against the people who hurt me, to not be able to do anything. I have the power to do something now though and I will not waste it. These people deserve to be treated better than they are. They deserve to be able to talk to people and have fun, to walk down the hall without having to worry about people messing with them. They deserve peace.

I continue walking to class with my head held high. Even though there is still water soaking the back of my shirt, I still remain strong and proud. I can hear a few people throw hurtful words at me, but I don't listen. They aren't worthy of my time. Soon, I will make them regret every single harsh word they ever said to someone. I will make them suffer.

Chapter Five
Colomba-
A Sweet Boy,
A Mean Girl

The bell rings shrilly and a huge crowd of students leave the classrooms to head to their next class, just like every day. My bag is stuffed full of books and it weighs me down a bit as I make my way through the halls. I weave through the crowd, trying to be careful and not hit anybody with my overstuffed bag. I guess having a super heavy bag is part of my punishment for taking so many advanced classes. Hey, at least it's helping me achieve my dream of going to a good college and all that, so I guess it will be worth it in the end. I suppose I can live with having a sore back for now. I just have to learn to suffer through it until high school is over.

My heavy bag bumps into my leg as I turn a corner. I just know I'm going to have a huge bruise on my leg because of this bag. I stop for a moment to rub the sore spot on my calf. As the pain slowly disappears, I overhear two people talking near me. I don't look over at them since I don't want it to look like I'm spying on them, but I can see two figures, a boy and a girl, standing beside the lockers from the corner of my eye. The gentle, nervous tone of one of them draws my attention and I listen in.

"I was just wondering if… if you're not busy or anything… would you like to go out with me one night? Maybe we could get dinner." I smile to myself as I hear this. Whoever this guy is, they just sounded so shy and sweet when they asked her, it was adorable. Apparently, whoever he is asking out doesn't think that this is cute though since I hear a cold, evil little laugh.

"Did you really think that I would ever go out with a fat tub of lard like you?" I turn around in surprise to hear someone say something so cruel. I am not surprised when I see who it was that said that, Angela.

Her snobby face is twisted into a grimace of disgust. She is looking up into the heartbroken eyes of Kal Kelvin. Even though Angela is a bit taller than me, she practically has to look straight up to look into Kal's pain filled face. He is one of the tallest guys in school. Kal is even taller than Luis, which is pretty amazing to me. Luis is super tall in my eyes. Kal may only be one of the tallest people in school, but when it comes to weight he is definitely the biggest. His belly hangs over his pants and jiggles with every movement he makes. His head is shaved, with his round body this almost makes him look like a giant bowling ball. With his huge body, he is a bit intimidating. Everyone who knows him though will admit that he is a complete sweetheart. This just makes it even worse to see him getting teased so mercilessly about his size. Angela isn't done with his torment though.

"If the two of us went out to eat, the restaurant would probably run out of food because you'll just shovel everything into that massive mouth of yours. I would have to be a complete idiot to let myself go through that embarrassment." It almost looks as if Kal is going to cry. I can't take this anymore. I've got to do something. I can't let her keep on hurting this poor guy just for asking her out. I step forward, forgetting about the pain in my leg.

"C'mon Angela, don't be a jerk. He was just trying to ask you out. It's not like he was asking you to help him murder a bunch of puppies or something. A simple no would have been fine." Angela rolls her eyes at me as if I am the one in the wrong here.

"Oh please Colomba. This giant creep needs to learn that no girl will go out with him because of how big he is. Face it, I'm doing him a favor by teaching him this." I glare at her, not understanding how somebody can be so stupid and mean.

"The only thing you're teaching anybody here is how much of snobby brat you are." Angela isn't even insulted by what I just said, she just laughs at me. Her laugh is cold, I almost want to smack the smirk off her face, but I know that would only make things worse for me. It's never a smart idea to hit the principal's daughter.

"C'mon Colomba, it's not like I'm doing anything bad by saying these things to him. I mean, somebody has to tell him what a fat pig he is or else he's never gonna learn, now is he? Somebody has to tell all these people what's wrong with them, and they're lucky that they're learning it from me." All of the anger leaves me as I stare at her in shock. Did she actually just say that? Did she actually just say that and mean it? From the superior way she is looking down at me, I'm guessing that the answer is yes. I stare at her for a moment, taking in a slow, deep breath to make sure I don't scream at her.

"I would say something mean back to you about how stupid you are acting, but I think you are easily showing everyone just how stupid you are by how you're acting right now." I look over at Kal, whose face is a deep red from embarrassment. "I wouldn't waste my time with a girl like her if I were you Kal, she doesn't deserve someone as nice as you." I walk away without another word.

How can Angela be so stupid and cruel? What is wrong with her? What makes her so special that she has the right to say those things to people? Is she so perfect that she has the job to point out everyone else's flaws to them? I can only hope that Kal will be okay, he looked so crushed when I left him. I can only imagine why he wanted to ask Angela out, if I liked girls, she would be the last one I would ever be interested in. Oh well, he may not have the best taste in girls, but he is still a very kind person and I can only hope that his little crush on her is gone after all that. I can only hope that he's smart enough to never care for another girl like her again.

The rest of the day just seems to fly by after that, but no matter what my mind seems to keep going back to what happened with Angela and Kal. I can't stop thinking about how hurt Kal looked. I should have done more for him. I really should have. I shouldn't have just left him there while he was still in pain. I just felt so aggravated though that I couldn't stay in front of Angela another minute.

It didn't make my annoyance go away after school when I had to stay after for an hour to tutor Alex in math. He kept staring at me and trying to flirt while I was explaining how to do a simple problem to him. I swear it's like pulling out teeth trying to get him to actually focus on math instead of me. I almost felt like letting out a sigh of relief when the hour was up, and I could go home.

My grandma was waiting for me outside and I practically leaped into the car to make sure Alex wouldn't catch up to me and try to keep talking. When she asked me how my day was, I immediately told her all about what happened with Angela and Kal. I don't even bother to hide my anger as I tell her about how cruel Angela was, thankfully Nonna doesn't say anything and lets me talk. I really needed to let this out or else I was going to explode. When I'm done telling her what happened, I still feel some anger left in me, as well as some questions that I ask her without a second thought.

"I don't get it. Why would Angela make fun of him for big like he is, I mean it's so normal?" My grandmother smiles at me sadly.

"It may be normal now, but it has only been like that recently. Not that long ago, being obese was a very strange thing. Practically everyone was skinny, and it was strange to see a bigger person. Nowadays it's the other way around. Now you see more bigger people than skinny ones."

"Yeah, so if it's normal now, why would she make fun of him?"

"Because, back when it wasn't normal, people thought very badly of people who were bigger. They thought of them as lazy and disgusting even though it may not have been true and that person could have been very kind, but it wouldn't matter. Sadly, people have passed on those beliefs to their children and now they think the same way. It is very sad how so many cruel things people can pass on to their children. Hopefully, one day, there will be no more hatred to pass on." My grandmother looks out the windshield of her car with a thoughtful expression and I know that I shouldn't disturb her by trying to continue the conversation, her mind is miles away.

I stare out the window, my mind wandering to many different things. I think about how mean Angela had been to a boy who was being kind to her. I think about what my grandmother said about how people used to think about people who are bigger. And I think about how unfair it is for these people to be treated so badly because of their size. As the world passes by us as my grandmother drives, I can't help but wonder how long it will take before there is no more hatred to pass on to the next generation. When I think about Angela, Alex, and all the kids who have been hurting others and saying cruel things about everyone around me, as well as Silver Dove, I just know that it will be a very long time before the world can have that kind of peace.

Chapter Six
Luis-
The Bake
Sale

Advanced Placement Art History is one of my favorite classes this year. Not only do I love art and my favorite teacher, Mr. Sizemore, is teaching it, but Colomba is in this class with me. No matter how bad my day is going, this class always makes me feel better.

Colomba is sitting beside me now, taking notes as Mr. Sizemore talks about the different periods in art history. I try to scribble down my notes as fast as possible as he talks, but Colomba seems to be having no problem keeping up with Mr. Sizemore's fast pace. While I'm busily scribbling my notes, the familiar irritating siren goes off over the intercom and everyone in the class seems to share the same annoyance with it. We have all gone through this many times before and we all know what it is, it's a Crow Drill. It's supposed to be practice for when I come around as the Crow and cause problems for everyone. Mr. Sizemore doesn't even have to tell everyone what to do, we know it all by heart now. Mr. Sizemore covers the glass on the door, locks it, and turns out the lights while the class cowers in the back corner, as if expecting someone to burst through the door at any second.

Mr. Sizemore may have helped with the lockdown like he's supposed to, but when he's done he doesn't make us stay silent like the principal said we should. Mr. Sizemore lets us whisper softly to each other. I guess that he thinks this drill is silly just like everyone else in this class. I'm about to start whispering to Colomba when I overhear a conversation between two people behind me.

"I can't believe that we have to do this stupid thing again. I swear we keep doing this more and more often. It's like they think this will actually do anything when the Crow shows up again. A locked door isn't going to stop him and whoever he transforms next, they'll just smash through it like it's paper." The guy talking just shakes his head. "Everybody knows that it's going to happen again, it's not as if Silver Dove really does anything. She makes them go away for a moment, but the Crow always comes back. It's almost as if she isn't really doing anything at all."

"I know right." The girl he is talking to responds, her voice full of annoyance. "It's like she's barely even trying. She just gets rid of whoever he transformed and calls it a day. I don't think she's even looking for him when he does appear. Maybe what everyone is saying is true, maybe they really are on the same side and they're just trying to make her look like the hero." The guy chuckles.

"Well, whatever is going on, I won't be cheering for Silver Dove anymore. It's obvious that if she hasn't been able to beat him this entire time, then the Crow is going to win one of these days. It's probably for the best to just join his side while we have the chance." I feel the corners of my mouth rise into a pleased smile.

Well, well, well, it seems that things are starting to look up for me. I've been hearing more and more people talking like this and I'm loving it. They are finally turning away from Silver Dove and are turning to me instead. They are turning to me more out of fear than respect like I wanted, but hey at least they are still turning to me, that's all I can ask for. I can feel my body straighten in pride. It kind of feels like I'm winning now, I'm finally beating Silver Dove at something. I smile as I look down at Colomba, eager to talk to her, but the smile disappears from my face as soon as I look at her. Her eyes are misted over, as if she is holding back tears while she stares ahead blankly, not really looking at anything at all.

What is she so sad about? What could cause her to cry like that so suddenly? It only takes me a moment to realize that she probably overheard that conversation too and it upset her. I have known for a long time that she is a fan of Silver Dove, but I didn't think that she cared so much that she would cry just from hearing someone say something mean about Silver Dove. I didn't realize that she is this sensitive. The happiness I had felt when I heard them talk immediately disappears at seeing her sad face. Reaching down, I rest my hand on her shoulder, she jumps a little in surprise. It's almost as if she completely forgot that she is in a room with a bunch of other people.

"Hey, are you okay?" I whisper to her. She quickly blinks away the tears clouding her eyes as she smiles up at me.

"Oh yeah, I'm fine. I just wish that we didn't have to do these things anymore. I wish the Crow would just leave us alone and things could stay sane for once." In her smile, I can see that it is fake. She is only smiling right now so that I won't be concerned about her. I want to question her a bit more, but the principal's voice comes over the intercom to announce that the drill is over and that we can go back to normal. When we have the classroom set up the way it's supposed to, the bell rings signaling the end of class.

I swipe my books off my desk while Colomba grabs her bag and the two of us walk out the door together. Even though we are walking side by side, she doesn't say anything. It's as if she is still thinking about what was said in the classroom. I try to smile at her, but I don't think it looks sincere, I'm too worried about her to have a real smile.

"Are you sure you're okay Colomba?" She smiles up at me sweetly.

"Yes, I swear I'm fine." Her eyes look past me, and a real smile finally comes over her face. "Oh hey, look." Colomba points behind me and I turn around to see a poster taped to the wall. On the poster it is talking about a big bake sale that the school will be having to earn money so that the debate team can afford to go to the state championship.

I glare at the poster as anger begins to rise in me. Oh, I see, the sports teams get everything they need from the school without any problems, but the academic teams have to work hard just so they can afford to go to a competition. A school is supposed to be a place where you learn, so shouldn't the academic teams get more money from the schools than the stupid sports teams? Even though I hate what this means, Colomba is smiling at the poster.

"That looks like it would be pretty fun." I don't really understand what she means until I take a closer look at the poster. Written near the bottom of the poster, it is asking for people to sign up and provide some baked goods to sell at the bake sale. I smile over at Colomba.

"You going to make some stuff for them?" Colomba chuckles at me.

"Well naturally. It's not like I'm going to give up a chance to show off my awesome baking skills." She says this in a teasing tone that makes me laugh.

"Well would you like some help with that?" She smiles up at me with joy.

"I would love that. Do you think we can meet up at the store sometime soon so that we can get the ingredients and everything?" I nod my head eagerly, barely believing that she said yes.

"Of course. Maybe I can even show you how to make some of the recipes my mother left behind that she brought over from Puerto Rico. I like making her recipes, she was apparently a really good cook. It's also fun to experiment with some of the recipes to make them your own." I start telling her about some of the recipes that my mother left behind when an unfriendly voice calls out from behind me.

"Why am I not surprised that a nerd like you likes baking Louie?" I feel my cheeks growing warm as I blush in embarrassment, I turn around to face Alex who is smiling at me as if he is a lion looking down on some prey it plans on killing. Colomba turns to face him too, but she isn't embarrassed like me, she is furious.

"And what is wrong with that Alex? I like baking too, does that mean there is something wrong with me too?" Alex actually takes a step back in surprise at seeing the intensity of the fire in her eyes, and her rage only seems to be building with each second that passes.

"W- Well of course not, Colomba. Nothing could ever be wrong with you." His smile returns as he glances up at me. "But you have to admit that a guy baking instead of a girl is pretty weird." I don't know how it's possible, but her glare somehow gets even darker.

"No, I don't "have to admit" anything like that. It is perfectly alright for a guy to bake too. It's not just something a woman can do. Hobbies and other stuff aren't just for boys or girls, you can like whatever you want to like." Alex chuckles at her as if she is being silly.

"That's nice to say, but I think everyone else in the world will agree with me when I say that Louie over there will look like a sissy when he puts on that apron and helps you make some cute cupcakes." He sneers at me while Colomba rolls her eyes.

"There is no point arguing with this idiot." I hear Colomba mumbling quietly under her breath before she speaks up so that she can address Alex. "We'll see you later Alex, we have places to be." Without another word, she turns back around and marches away with me walking beside her and leaving Alex behind with a surprised stare directed at Colomba and I. I chuckle for a second before I catch up to Colomba who is marching down the hall in her rage. When I am walking beside her again, she doesn't even look at me as she practically growls a question at me.

"Can you believe he said something like that? I mean, that has to be one of the most ridiculous things I've heard in a long time!" I shrug.

"Honestly, it doesn't surprise me. I hear him say stuff like that all the time. Maybe he just doesn't say stuff like that around you as often because he likes you and he doesn't want to look bad to you." She stops suddenly and I have to take a few steps back since I didn't expect that and walked past her. She looks as if I just said something that surprised her. Colomba starts walking again, but this time at her normal pace.

"I guess you're right. I didn't really think about that, I guess guys say a lot of things around other guys that they would never say to a girl they like." I smile at her. She surprises me sometimes. Colomba is a really smart girl, but she is really naive too. She has a very innocent mind. Whenever she shows her innocent side like this, it makes me want to protect her from all the bad things in this world. I never want her to be hurt, I don't want her to lose her beautiful innocence.

We talk about the bake sale until I drop her off at her next class. According to the poster there will be a meeting after school tomorrow for all the people who want to participate in the bake sale. Colomba and I agreed that we would both be there. As I sit down in my next class, I fantasize over what I hope it will be like to spend a day baking with Colomba. The teacher starts teaching, but I barely pay attention. My mind is too wrapped up thinking beautiful thoughts of Colomba.

Chapter Seven
Colomba-
Kal

School ended just a few minutes ago, but I am staying behind to do some tutoring. Alex is the only one I tutor right now while the others in the tutoring program help at least two or three people. I don't think anybody else in the program has any hard feelings about this though since I think all of us silently know that Alex is a handful and needs to have some special attention.

I'm sitting in one of the science classrooms now waiting for him to arrive. Alex is always a few minutes late, no matter what. It's super annoying, but I've gotten used to it at this point. I get paid well for this little job, so I don't mind a few small annoyances.

As I shuffle through some of my papers, I glance up to see a familiar face. That guy I had seen the other day who tried to ask Angela out, Kal. He is walking into the room, his feet shuffling nervously on the floor. It's only at this moment that I remember that I have seen him in this tutoring program before. I think he gets tutored in biology or something like that. He walks over to a table with a big display of DNA made up of colorful beads where his tutor is currently talking to a girl who is also a tutor. Kal asks if they can start tutoring, but his tutor just glares at him, angry that he interrupted his conversation. The tutor tells him to just be patient and give him a moment to finish what he was saying. He says this with so much venom in his voice that I'm surprised Kal doesn't look more hurt by it. A dark thought enters my mind, I've heard that he is bullied a lot, he is probably used to being treated like that.

As Kal turns around to find a seat, his large stomach bumps into the DNA display and it falls to the ground with a crash. The beads that made up the DNA display scatter all over the floor. Kal closes his eyes and lowers his head as he lets out a soft groan of embarrassment and misery.

"Look what you did now you stupid fat pig. If you weren't such a fat creep this wouldn't have happened." Kal turns away from the guy who said this and walks out the door, his feet dragging on the ground, scattering some of the beads across the room.

My heart feels as if it is crumbling in my chest. He looks as if he is slowly dying on the inside. I follow after him without a second thought. When I make it to the doorway, I can see that he is walking out the back exit of the school that leads to the teacher's parking lot. I maneuver my way through the crowd before I make it through the door. Inside there was a constant buzz of noise from the other students, out here there is only the peaceful chirp of birds and what sounds like the crinkling of a plastic wrapper. I look over to where the noise came from to see Kal sitting on the ground with his back against the wall, trying to open up the wrapper to a candy bar.

"Hey Kal." He glares up at me, angry that I'm interrupting him.

"Hey." His voice is an angry growl, but I know that he is not angry with me. He is angry about what happened. I kneel down beside him as he continues to struggle to open the wrapper.

"I'm sorry about what happened in there. Are you alright?"

"Yeah, I'm fine." It's easy to see that he is not fine. He looks so frustrated that he might just rip apart the candy bar he is having so much trouble opening.

"Would you like some help opening that?" He glares at me for a moment and I suddenly feel bad for asking. I think that I just hurt his pride.

"No, I don't need your help. I'll just eat this, and I'll be fine." I look at him fumble with the candy bar, his anger making him clumsy.

"Do you really think that eating that will make you feel better?" He stops messing with the candy bar and glares at me again.

"It's what I do when I'm upset. I eat when I'm upset, it makes me feel better." Even though his voice is full of anger, I keep my voice calm when I speak to him.

"It may make you feel better at the moment, but it won't take away the problem. They make fun of you for being bigger than them, eating more will only make the problem worse." He looks away from me to stare out at the parking lot.

"You think I don't know that? You think I'm an idiot, don't you? Everyone else seems to think that too." He looks over at me and chuckles coldly. "I don't expect you to understand. You've probably been small your entire life. You don't have the problems I have. You don't have to deal with people constantly thinking that you're lazy and stupid just because you're bigger than them. People constantly make fun of me even though I have never done a thing to them." His hands quiver a little in his fury before he shakes his head and stands up. "I'm done with this! Leave me alone!" Without another word he marches off, leaving me by myself, feeling like I've failed.

My head hangs low as I make my way back to the classroom. When I enter the classroom, I can see that Alex has finally arrived. He smiles up at me mischievously, as if he just caught me doing something wrong.

"Well, well look who's late." I want to snap at him and point out the obvious that he's always late while this is my first time, but I don't. I take in a deep breath to calm myself down before I speak, and I sit down beside him.

"Sorry about that Alex, but I needed to talk to Kal." Jealousy suddenly flashes in his eyes and his next words come out with a little bit of a growl in it.

"What was so important that you had to be with him instead of with me like you were supposed to?" I feel my muscles tense as I hear the harsh words. I glare at him as I give him my answer.

"Some of the others were making fun of him because he's big, so I was trying to comfort him." Alex immediately relaxes, the jealous look in his eyes fading. He chuckles at me as if I am being ridiculous.

"Oh c'mon Colomba, don't worry about making that tub of lard feel better. He deserves to feel that way since he let himself get that fat. A guy should never let himself get like that. A guy needs to be strong so that he can protect his girl." He tries to wrap his arm around me, but I move out of his reach. I glare at him, feeling my anger boiling inside of me.

"Alex if you are going to keep saying cruel things like that then you can find somebody else to tutor you because I won't stand for it." His cool and collected look is shattered as he suddenly looks very worried.

"Oh hey, it's alright! I didn't mean anything by that!" I still don't release him from my glare.

"Well, if you don't mean anything by it, then don't say it. Now can we just get started, I would rather not spend our tutoring hour arguing." He nods with a hurt look on his face, but I don't bother to comfort him. Instead, we go over how to find the areas of different shapes. Thankfully, he stays silent today so as soon as the hour is up, I rush outside where my grandmother is waiting in the car. The two of us immediately start talking about how our day was, but I don't tell her about what happened with Kal. I still feel too disappointed to talk about it. The countryside passes by our car as we make our way home. I usually enjoy looking at the scenery when we drive, but today I don't, I don't even pay attention. My mind is a million miles away, busy thinking about all that happened today and how Alex acted when I told him about Kal. By the time we make it home, my muscles are tensed in anger and I have to head straight to my room to make sure that I won't be unpleasant to my grandma or dad since they had nothing to do with why I'm angry. I close the door to my room and lie down on my bed, trying to make my racing thoughts slow down. No matter what I do though, my thoughts keep circling back to what happened, and I keep thinking about how I should have done more.

Chapter Eight
Luis-
The Meeting

The final bell is ringing, but Colomba and I aren't heading out the doors like everyone else. We are heading to the meeting for the people who want to help out with the bake sale for the debate team. She looks so happy as we walk to the room. Her aquamarine eyes sparkle like the jewels they are. I'm glad that she has cheered up a bit. At lunch today, she was a bit upset since she was telling me about how she had tried to comfort a guy I have seen around before named Kal, but he was rude and blew her off. When she told me that I felt very angry, I wanted to find Kal and tell him off for being so rude to a sweet girl like Colomba when she was only trying to help. I knew that Colomba would be upset with me for doing that though, so I held that back.

We enter the classroom where the meeting is being held to find the debate team there along with a few others who are going to be helping out. The meeting won't start for another few minutes, so Colomba and I find a seat and we start talking. As

Colomba tells me about something weird she saw earlier today, I notice somebody enter the room. It's that guy Kal that Colomba told me about earlier, the one she tried to comfort yesterday when she was tutoring. He glances around, looking very uncomfortable, and sits down by himself on the other side of the room from Colomba and I.

I have seen Kal before, but I've never really talked to him. A lot of people have made fun of him for being fat as long as I have known him. Life must be pretty difficult for him, being so much bigger than everybody else. I hear people call him many names that aren't very nice; pig, blob, and giant are just a few of them.

The head of the debate team, Missy Marson, stands at the front of the classroom and clears her throat as she adjusts her glasses nervously to look at everyone.

"Hi everyone, thanks for coming and agreeing to help us with the bake sale. We are going to pass around a sheet of paper, and we want you to write down your names and what you plan on making and then we will discuss it and come up with prices for everything." She passes a piece of paper to the person sitting next to her who starts writing down what they'll bring. The paper makes its way around the room until it reaches Colomba. She smiles cheerfully as she writes down that she will be making cupcakes. She hands the paper to me and I write dulce de coco, a traditional Latin American dessert that my mom left a recipe behind for me that I love to make for myself. It kind of looks like a coconut macaroon and kind of tastes like one too.

They are one of my favorite sweet snacks.

When I hand the paper to the girl next to me, I hear them whisper something to their friend. "Too bad Kal is here. I bet as soon as our backs are turned, he will gobble up everything we make for this sale." The two girls giggle while I feel my body tense in anger. They are such snobby little brats to tease him like that when I bet he hasn't said a mean word to either of them in his life. What is wrong with these people in this school? Sometimes it feels that Colomba, Nat, and I are the only sane ones left here.

It's not too long after that that everyone has signed the paper and put down what they are going to make. The paper is returned to Missy and everyone discusses what they are making, and a price is decided for each item. This only takes an hour to do and Missy tells us before we all leave that we will be meeting an hour before the sale is supposed to start so that we can all help set up. With that said, she dismisses everyone, and we all head out the door.

Everyone rushes by us while Colomba and I walk at a slow pace. I look down at her sweet face and swallow my fear so that I can ask her something I have been dying to do.

"Hey, how about we meet up Sunday morning and get some of the ingredients and then make this stuff? Do you want to?" I smile at her, my heart racing.

"Sure, I'd love to do that. Maybe we can hang out and make some of the stuff afterward." She smiles sweetly at me.

"That sounds like fun, I can't wait." My heart is pounding in my chest. Is this a date? Did I just ask her out on a date, and she said yes? I feel like I just died and went to heaven. Colomba grins up at me mischievously.

"I bet that I can sell more of my cupcakes than your coconut things." I grin back down at her.

"You think so?" She puts her hands on her hips and faces me.

"I know so, I'm totally going to kick your butt at this."

"Oh really?"

"Yes, really."

"And just how do you know that?"

"You just reek of failure."

"Really? What does failure smell like?" She sniffs the air teasingly.

"Cologne."

"You do know that this is the cologne you bought me for my birthday, right?" I ask her, pretending to be insulted.

"I'm sorry, I didn't realize I bought you essence of failure." She walks ahead of me, trying to hide her grin, I don't bother to hide mine. I'm too happy to hide that. The two of us walk outside where my uncle is waiting in his car to drive the two of us home. I know that when we drop her off home and I tell him about my date with Colomba, he's going to tease me the rest of the day about it, but I don't care. Nothing can bother me today. Right now, I am as invincible as Silver Dove.

After we have dropped Colomba home and my uncle spends the rest of the drive teasing me like I suspected after I tell him about my date with Colomba, we make it home and I immediately head straight for my room. I toss my backpack onto my bed and place my hand on top of my Crow Medal. Shadow appears, perched on top of my painting easel. She fluffs out her feathers for a moment, as if I just woke her up from a nap, before she looks at me with warmth in her dark, black eyes.

"Good evening Master, judging from the smile on your face, I'm guessing this is a very good evening." I chuckle at her.

"Of course it's a very good evening. Didn't you hear, I'm going out on a date with Colomba this weekend and we're going to bake together." Now it's Shadow's turn to chuckle at me.

"Yes, I am aware that you two will be meeting up, but is it a date? Did Colomba say that this is going to be a date, or are you just hoping that it is?" I feel myself rolling my eyes even though I didn't really mean to.

"C'mon Shadow, it's a date. Stop trying to make me feel bad." Shadow shrugs her wings at me.

"Sorry, I just don't want you to get your hopes up for nothing. There is something else on your mind though, isn't there? I can sense it." I lower my eyes from hers. I was thinking about something else, something that was making some of my happiness fade. Colomba had been telling me about what happened the other day when she was tutoring. She saw Kal getting picked on and tried to comfort him, but he snapped at her. When she went back inside to tutor Alex, he told her some more mean things about Kal and people who are big like him that made her even more upset.

"Yeah, I do have something else on my mind. Earlier today, Colomba was telling me about how she had tried to help Kal after some people had made fun of him and he got mad at her. Then she talked to Alex about it and he made her even more upset. He basically told her that a guy needs to be strong like him so that they can defend the girl they like." I glance down at my thin, not muscular arms and I feel a bit embarrassed. I guess that if Alex is right about the world, then I'm a pathetic guy since Colomba could definitely defend herself better than I could ever defend her. She would honestly be the one defending me. I feel my face growing warm at the thought and I know that I am blushing. Shadow shakes her head slowly.

"Yes, I am not surprised that someone with as small a mind as Alex would say something like that. Sometimes it surprises me to remember that you two used to be friends." My hands instantly turn into fists at that memory.

"Only as kids." I hear myself growl under my breath. "I would never even want to be friendly to that guy now after everything he's done. He can go die in a hole for all I care." Shadow flies off my easel and onto my shoulder. Using her beak, she gently pushes my bangs out of my face.

"I'm sorry Master, I didn't mean to upset you by bringing back those bad memories." I take in a few deep breaths to help myself relax.

"It's alright Shadow, I understand. You didn't mean anything by it."

"Alex has been such an ignorant child; it

doesn't surprise me that he believes that widely held belief. He doesn't give himself a chance to think differently than everyone else." I look over at her, feeling a bit confused.

"What are you talking about Shadow?" She looks into my eyes, with her being on my shoulder, our eyes are only an inch or two away from each other's. When I look into her black eyes so closely, it is almost scary. They are intelligent eyes, in her eyes I can see that she is more intelligent than I will ever be, maybe even more intelligent than anyone else on earth.

"When a person is not very smart, they just believe all of the things that most people say. They go with the crowd. Sadly, what everyone else thinks isn't always the right thing. This is like how Alex, and everyone else, is viewing this boy Kal." I lower my eyebrows in confusion.

"Explanation please?" Shadow closes her dark eyes as she chuckles softly.

"People are controlled by their opinions. Most people share the same popular opinion since they don't give themselves the chance to think for themselves. These kids in your school are following the same beliefs as everyone else when thinking about this boy Kal and how big he is. People's opinions of obesity have changed many times over the years, and I have seen it happen. Centuries ago, being bigger was seen as a good thing, it meant that you were smart and knew how to survive so you had more food than everyone else. People looked up to you and asked for your advice so that they could be successful like them. Things changed though when food became something that you could easily get. After that, if you were bigger people thought of you as lazy and you ate too much. After that, the view hasn't really changed. It has been like this for a long time now. To be obese was once considered beautiful, but now it is attractive to be incredibly skinny. The strange part is that obesity is becoming a more common thing in this world, yet people still make fun of others for it. It is very strange, but then again, humans are very strange." I think about what she said for a minute before I chuckle.

"Yeah, you're right. People are strange." I walk over to my window and look at the downtown street below me. It is a pretty street with old historical buildings, not a bustling city street at all, but a pleasant small town main street. People are busily moving from one place to another, not really paying attention to anything else besides the task they are trying to do. As I watch these people, I think about Kal.

Kal seems like a pretty nice guy but has always been seen as the "fat kid" in our school, even when we were little. The poor guy just never could catch a break. Even though I feel bad for him since everyone is making fun of him, I can't help but be angry with him too. I mean, I get made fun of just because I'm alive, but he has control over the reason he gets made fun of. He can just lose some weight and he would be normal, and nobody would mess with him. I lower my head, feeling ashamed of myself. I'm the Crow, I'm supposed to be standing up for the other bullied kids, not joining the bullies' side. Kal probably has tried to lose weight before and it hasn't worked yet. Judging by how often people tease him about his weight, he's probably tried a billion times to lose weight. The poor guy would probably need a lot of help to lose all that extra weight he has.

I smile as the obvious suddenly comes into my mind. I may be the kind of help he needs. I may not be able to help him lose weight, but the Crow can help him with his problem dealing with other people. Oh yes, the Crow can definitely help him with that. I can make the world fear him, make them wish they had never hurt him at all. I glance over at Shadow, who is staring out the window with a peaceful gaze. She wouldn't like it I were to transform Kal, but I know that she wouldn't argue with me. She has been letting me use my powers the way I like without nagging me like she used to. Maybe that is what I need to do, just transform him. It has been a while since the Crow has shown up, they may need to be reminded that I am still here and ready to fight.

I watch the sun set in the distance as I try to think about what I should do about Kal, but once the sun has disappeared and darkness has fallen, I still haven't made my decision.

Chapter Nine
Colomba-
Luis Stands Up

The morning sun is shining brightly through the windows in the school hallway as Luis, Nat, and I walk through the halls to head to our first classes. We chat and laugh as we wander through the maze of hallways, and Nat leaves Luis and I alone to go down a different hall. Now that it's just the two of us, we start talking about the bake sale and the things we plan on making. He wants to make a traditional dessert from Puerto Rico that has coconut in it which sounds super good. When he is done explaining to me what his dessert is, I tell him what type of cupcake I plan on making.

"I want to make red velvet cupcakes. They are one of my favorite things to make. When they are done baking, you scoop out part of the inside and you fill it with marshmallow cream and then cover the top with cream cheese frosting. It is so good and so much fun to make. It takes a lot of work to make it from scratch, but it's worth it." I hear someone laugh coldly at my side. Luis looks over there and his smile instantly disappears into a dark glare. I glance over as well to see that Angela is the one laughing at us. My smile fades too as she stops laughing and looks at me with a superior smirk on her face. Angela flips her blonde hair dramatically over her shoulder.

"Why am not surprised that a freak like you has such an old lady hobby like baking?" I'm about to open my mouth and say something back to her when someone else beats me to the punch. I'm surprised to find that the person standing up for me is Luis.

"At least she has a talent, unlike you." I'm shocked by his words, but my shock is nothing compared to Angela's. Her tanned face grows so red that it looks like she might explode at any second. Her lips are pursed into a tight, thin line. After a moment of tense silence, Angela opens her mouth as if she is about to yell at Luis before she closes her mouth again and turns on her heels to march down the hallway in a huff. She walks straight through a group of people and they have to scatter out of her way to avoid getting plowed into. Looking up at Luis, he is glaring at Angela's retreating figure with a defiant stare.

Oh my gosh! I have never seen Luis do anything like that before. He's usually terrified whenever someone like Angela or Alex is around him. He isn't terrified right now though. Right now, he looks furious. His hands are clenched into tight fists at his side. It's not until Angela is out of sight when she turns the corner that he finally looks away from her and smiles down at me. His smile is a little awkward since he appears to be a bit embarrassed by what just happened.

"Sorry about that, I probably sounded like a complete jerk." I can't help it, I laugh.

"It- it's okay Luis." Each word is interrupted by a giggle, but I somehow manage to calm myself so that I can continue speaking. "I have never seen you do something like that before. Did you see her face? She looked as if you called her every bad name in the book. That was awesome!" I start laughing all over again, Luis stares down at me for a moment in confusion before he laughs along with me.

The two of us continue to walk down the hall to our next class, talking and laughing about what just happened. Angela's shocked face will always be in my mind, and I love it. I can never forget that. I only wish that I could have taken a picture of that to show Nat. Angela has always been mean to us, as well as everyone else. It was so great to see her like that. It's probably not a nice thing to think, but after all the terrible things she has done to everyone, it is nice to see her have a taste of her own medicine.

It doesn't take long before I leave Luis at his next class while I walk two doors down to get to mine. When I am almost through the door, I hear two familiar voices talking, I don't really pay attention until I hear them talk about Silver Dove and I stop dead in my tracks.

"I don't know what to think about Silver Dove anymore. I mean, think about it, she never *really* defeats the Crow, she lets him go every single time. It's just stupid." The voice belongs to a girl I know named Rebecca who is in my math class. She is talking to one of her friends, Emily. "If she was a real hero, she would stop him forever and she wouldn't have let this go on for so long." Emily looks at her friend, a bit embarrassed as she tries to defend me.

"But she is trying to help, isn't she? She tries to stop him every time he shows up." Rebecca only rolls her eyes at that.

"Yeah, but only after he has one of the people he transforms wreck everything and scare everyone. Maybe she should just give up. The Crow is obviously going to defeat her someday. One of the people he transforms won't give in to her one day and they will destroy her, so she might as well just quit." Emily hangs her head, defeated.

"I guess you're right." They walk past me, not knowing that they just walked past the girl they insulted.

They think I should give up? I have been hearing so may people say this about me recently, why do they think this after all I have done? Back when I first started as Silver Dove, Rebecca and Emily were two of my biggest supporters. Now my supporters are turning their backs on me. What could I have done differently so that they wouldn't turn away from me like this? Could I have done anything differently?

The Crow is so clever, I never know where to find him when he is causing trouble, so I can't stop him permanently like they want me to. I also can't just look for him when someone he has transformed is causing trouble, I need to protect the people they are trying to hurt. Can't they realize that I can't do everything? Can't they see that I can't be everywhere at once? Can't they see that I am trying my best? When I think about what they said though, I know that they can't see that. They don't want to see. They don't care.

I hide my tears as I walk through my classroom door. They did bring up a good point. Why do I keep fighting him even though I will probably never really defeat him, and he will one day transform someone who won't back down? Nonna once said that the Crow is more powerful than me, maybe it's just silly for me to think I can keep this up forever. One day he will win, and I can only imagine what will happen when he does.

I sit down at my desk, laying my head down on it so nobody can see me cry. I cry because I know that I will face defeat one day, maybe one day soon. I cry because the people who once cheered for me are now turning away from me. And I cry because I feel as if I am truly alone even though I am surrounded by people. The teacher starts the class, but this is one of the only times that I don't pay attention to them. I am too miserable to even try. Luis may have been able to defend me from Angela, but he couldn't defend me from those girls in the hall. I am Silver Dove though, I should be able to defend myself, but I can't. I can't defeat the Crow, and I can't even defend myself from all of these people around me who have started to doubt me. I can't do anything right.

Chapter Ten
Luis-
Baking

My Uncle Diego is driving down a long country road, leading to Colomba's house. The day has come for us to bake everything for the sale together. We decided that my uncle will drive us to the store to get the ingredients, her grandmother will pick us up, and then we will come back to her house to make everything. Sitting on my lap is the recipe book my mom made. In it she has all the recipes that she brought with her from Puerto Rico. It's both a happy and sad feeling to hold something that belonged to her. It's happy since it is a part of her, but it is sad since it is a part of my mother, a mother that I never really got to know before she and my dad died.

I push those depressing thoughts out of my head when I realize that we are turning into Colomba's driveway. As we go down Colomba's drive, I see her sitting on the rope swing, swinging gently with her eyes closed. She has a soft smile that is full of peace. I make sure to lock that image in my mind. With her like that and her beautiful flower covered house behind her, this would make an amazing painting. As soon as she hears the car, she opens her eyes to smile at us. She gives us a cheerful wave as she hops off the swing and walks toward our car. The second my uncle stops the car I pop open my door to greet her.

"Hey Colomba, how's it going?" She's wearing a little pink dress that makes her look so cute. I try not to stare at her, but it's almost impossible.

"Going good. Thanks for giving me a lift."

"No problem, happy to do it."

"You're so sweet. Nat should be meeting us at the store, her parents are dropping her off there." It feels like someone just punched me in the gut. I thought that it was just going to be the two of us. Kind of like a date. Apparently, I was wrong. This is just the three of us hanging out as friends. I open the car door for her, and she steps inside. Even though I feel a bit disappointed, I won't let that ruin my day. I get to hang out with her all day, today will be great. I just wish that Nat wasn't going to spend today with us.

Colomba and I talk the entire way to the store while my uncle silently smiles with amusement as he drives. My uncle drops us off in front before he heads off to do some other errands. He reminds us that we need to be standing outside for Colomba's grandmother in an hour, so we won't keep her waiting. We tell him that we won't forget, and he drives off. It only takes a few minutes for Nat to arrive and we all go through the automatic doors into the supermarket.

The three of us walk through the aisles, chatting about random stuff and laughing at each others' jokes. When we go through the aisle for spices, Colomba tries to reach up for one of the ingredients she needs, but even when she stands on her toes, she can't reach the bottle of vanilla. I chuckle softly before I step over to her and easily grab the bottle. Colomba smiles at me softly while a faint blush forms on her cheeks.

"Thanks for helping the shorty of the group."

"I don't think you're short, you're just… petite." Colomba chuckles.

""Petite", the nice way of saying short." She laughs teasingly. "Don't worry, I don't mind being short. It can be a bit annoying at times, but I'm used to it." Even though she is laughing about it now, I know that this is something that really bothers her. She is a very strong martial artist, but she is very small, and people think that she is weak and always needs help because of it. I've seen how hurt she looks when people, especially Alex, tell her that she needs help even though she and I both know that she could easily do those things on her own. I don't think I hurt Colomba's feelings though since she is smiling at me and telling me about a family of foxes that have made a little burrow near her house. She says that she can watch the little babies playing from her bedroom window.

When we have gathered everything we need to make her cupcakes and my dulce de coco, we take our ingredients to the checkout line to pay for it. The grumpy lady at the register scans all of our items and then we pay her, all of us avoiding her dark gaze since her angry eyes seem to glare right into our souls as she bags up all of our things.

I look over at Colomba as she takes two of the bags of ingredients while I get the rest. I want to be the one to bake with her, just the two of us. The problem is that I am stuck with one other person. I glance over at Nat and she glances back at me with a knowing look.

"Hey guys, I think I'm going to have to head home. I'm not feeling that well." Colomba's face immediately shows her concern.

"Are you okay Nat?"

"Oh yeah, just a bad headache. Nothing to get worried about." Colomba's smile returns slightly as most of her worry disappears.

"Good. Can you make it home alright?"

"Sure, I'll just call my mom. You guys go on and I'll see you later." She walks off, leaving Colomba and I alone. I smile as I watch her, I think I understand what just happened. Nat knows how I feel about Colomba, and I think she knew that I wanted to be alone with Colomba so she made up that excuse so that we could do that. I swear it's like she can read minds. I totally owe her one.

Nat's mom picks her up a few minutes later and then Colomba's grandmother picks us up only a minute or two after that. Colomba and I pile all of the ingredients into the trunk of the car and then get in the back seats. The two of us chat with her grandmother as she drives. Colomba's grandmother is a very sweet woman. Her hair is snowy white and cut short. I can see that Colomba got her eyes from her grandmother since her grandmother's eyes are the same beautiful aquamarine blue. Even though her skin is wrinkled, there is still a joyful beauty in her face. When I look at her, I suddenly realize that I am probably seeing what Colomba will look like fifty to sixty years from now. To me, she will still be just as beautiful as she is today.

In what seems like only seconds, we pull into Colomba's driveway and we pull all the stuff out of the trunk and head inside. We head straight to the kitchen and set all the stuff down on the counter. Colomba opens a drawer and pulls out two aprons. She puts a red one on and I can tell that it was made specifically for her since, at the top, the word Tesoro is embroidered along with a little rabbit. Colomba has told me that Tesoro is the nickname her grandmother has for her, it means treasure or darling. The one she is handing me must be her grandmother's. It is pink and a bit frilly. I put it on even though I feel really weird. I know that Alex would never let me forget this if he saw me, he would probably take a picture to show everyone at school. Colomba doesn't seem bothered by it or try to tease me, so I let it go. I'm lucky enough to be doing this with her, I shouldn't complain.

We get busy, starting with Colomba's cupcakes. I start heating up the oven and getting the cupcake pan ready while Colomba starts mixing up some of the ingredients. When I am done with my little tasks, she asks me to measure out some flour and put it in the bowl while she mixes it. I carefully put just the right amount of flour into the measuring cup while the world seems to fall silent around us. Colomba stirs the mixture in the bowl while I slowly pour the flour in. I glance over at her, watching her concentrate on mixing. She looks so peaceful and sweet, I want to say something nice to her, but I can't figure out what to tell her. At moments like this I am jealous of Alex, he has the confidence to say whatever he wants around girls, but I can never tell Colomba what I really want to say. In my distraction, I let a large amount of the flour pour out all at once and a puff of flour flies out and sprinkles all over the front of Colomba's apron. She stares down at the dusting of flour all over her front and I feel my insides twisting in my embarrassment. Slick move genius, now you look like an even bigger dork to her. With a movement so quick I barely even see it, she dipped her hand into the bag of flour, grabbed a little bit of it, and gently threw it at my face with a giggle. I laugh and I feel some of the flour falling off my cheeks.

"Oh, you think that's funny, do you?" She giggles again.

"Yes, very funny."

"Well I'll show you then." I take a little bit of flour in my hand and toss it at her face, covering her nose and mouth. She takes in a little gasp before she laughs again.

"You're so gonna get it!" Colomba takes a handful of flour and throws it at me, making my black shirt almost look white. Before I know it, the two of us are throwing flour at each other, laughing in joy. The air is filled with the white powder, almost as if it is snowing inside Colomba's kitchen.

"What on earth is going on here?" The flour immediately stops flying as the two of us look over to see Colomba's dad standing in the doorway, his eyes narrowed in confusion. I glance over at Colomba, she is covered from head to toe in flour. Even her dark hair is white, she almost looks like a ghost. I bet that I probably look the same. Colomba looks at her father and gives him a nervous giggle.

"Baking." Her father smiles as he chuckles softly.

"Okay, just make sure that you clean up after yourselves." He leaves us alone, but I can still hear him chuckling as he makes his way down that hallway. Colomba glances over at me and laughs.

"You look like a bakery exploded on you." I laugh with her.

"Well you look like a ghost." I tease, and she just chuckles.

"Am I at least a scary ghost?" I chuckle right back at her.

"Yes, you are the most terrifying thing I've ever seen. You should star in your own scary movie." She giggles softly.

"Thanks, we should probably clean this up before my grandmother gets back. She hates having a messy kitchen and I don't think she would let us ever come back in here if she saw this mess." I smile as I nod at her.

We clean the flour off of everything and continue preparing the sweets. Colomba has to help me a lot since she has a lot more experience with being in the kitchen than I do. When it is time to make my dessert though, I have to show Colomba how to do some things and she listens eagerly to everything I tell her. Her bright blue eyes shine brightly in her curiosity as I tell her about some of the other recipes my mother left behind while we prepare the dulce de coco.

It feels like I just blinked one second and when I opened my eyes the desserts were all made and packed up for the bake sale tomorrow. The sun is beginning to set outside the kitchen window, and I know that it's time for my uncle to come pick me up. I grab my stuff and the two of us head out her front door.

Colomba and I watch my uncle's car come down her driveway as I hold a plastic container with the dulce de coco we made. She waves goodbye to me as I walk toward the car and open the door. My Uncle Diego's eyes grow wide as he looks at me, my hair still snowy white from the flour. As soon as he gets over the shock, he chuckles at me.

"Well look at you. What did you get yourself into Tigre?" I smile back at him, still bursting with happiness.

"Colomba and I were baking and… um… stuff happened." He laughs again.

"Apparently so. It looks like you both had a really good time."

"Yeah we did. I had the best time ever." I sigh softly and lean my head back against the seat. Wow, I never thought that I could ever be this happy. It feels as if every problem I've ever had is gone. If someone had told me that something like this would happen around three years ago, I wouldn't have believed them. I would have thought that the person telling me that was trying to mess with me. Back then, I wouldn't have believed that I deserve to be this happy. Back then, I thought that I was a loser who would never be happy. Things are changing though. Now I know that I deserve to be happy, everyone does. Colomba has shown me that. Ever since I started hanging out with her and I got my powers, things have been changing for the better for me. I see my life in a new way. I'm not going to stop fighting as the Crow though. Things might be a little better for me, but it doesn't mean that everything is perfect. People still mess with me all the time and it's a miracle if I can make it down the hallway alone without someone doing something to me. I see the same stuff happen to a bunch of other people in school too. I see it all the time, like what happened with Kal the other day. I will make this end so that all of us can finally have some peace, so that we can finally be free.

Chapter Eleven
Colomba-
Before the
Bake Sale

School passes quickly and when the final bell rings Luis and I are rushing to the assigned classroom where we will be having the last meeting before the bake sale starts. Tonight, our school will be having a basketball game where we will be selling the baked goods before, during half time, and after the game. Since we are all participating in the sale, we get to go to the game for free. I'm not a fan of sports, but it will be nice to see everyone happy and enjoying themselves. I might even learn how the sport is played since all I really know about basketball is that you try to get the ball in the hoop. Most people would suggest you just ask a guy friend to explain sports stuff to you, but my best guy friend is Luis and I think he knows less about sports than I do.

Luis and I enter the room with our three containers of desserts. Everyone else in the group has already arrived and it looks as if Missy is about to start our final meeting. The two of us sit down beside each other as Missy starts talking. She tells us when each of us will be assigned to man the bake sale table while the rest of the group is enjoying the game. With that said she asks if there are any questions before we start setting up the bake sale table. I raise my hand silently.

"Yes Colomba, what is it?" I stand up with a happy smile on my face.

"I made some extra cupcakes for everyone and I was hoping that I could pass them out before we start." Everyone gives me a little cheer while Missy smiles and nods.

I start handing out the extra red velvet cupcakes to everyone while Luis helps me by handing everyone a napkin to go with it. Luis is grinning so happily as he passes out the napkins, he is smiling at me as if he has never been this happy before in his life. When I think about how I've had my suspicions about Luis being picked on and bullied a lot, I can't help but think that I may be right. This may be the happiest he's ever been. Well, if this is the happiest he's ever been, I'm glad that I am the one helping him have this happy moment.

When all the cupcakes have been handed out, a sudden feeling comes over me that tells me that something bad is about to happen. I glance over at Kal. He has been busy getting the plate of his dessert, some chocolate chip cookies, ready to sell, so he hasn't eaten his cupcake yet. It is still sitting on the napkin on his desk. A guy has noticed this since he comes up from behind Kal with an evil grin on his face. The guy quickly snatches the cupcake off of Kal's napkin while Kal looks at him with disbelief.

"Hey that's mine!" He says this with his pain clearly being shown in his voice. The guy just scoffs at him.

"Trust me, with how big you are, you don't need this." Without wasting a second, the guy takes a bite out of the cupcake with that dark grin still on his face. Kal just watches him walk away with the cupcake with his mouth hanging slightly open, completely in shock by the cruelty of that guy.

I watch, stunned into silence by what just happened. I can't believe that guy just took Kal's cupcake like that. What is wrong with that guy? What is wrong with everyone else? I wonder this because I can see that almost everyone else in the room noticed what happened and they are chuckling about it, as if what just happened is funny.

Kal just keeps staring at that guy too as he finishes off the cupcake, also stunned into silence. The guy seems to enjoy his shock since he just laughs at Kal as he tosses the cupcake wrapper into the trash like a basketball and starts licking the icing off his fingers. When it looks as if Kal is about to cry, I finally break out of my shock and go up to him.

"It's okay Kal, I made extra so you can have another one." Kal's sadness quickly morphs into rage.

"You don't have to baby me Colomba, I don't need one your stupid cupcakes!" I feel myself move back a little in shock at hearing him speak so coldly to me. Why is he being so mean to me when I'm just trying to help? What did I do wrong?

"Okay, I'm sorry Kal. I didn't mean anything by it." I say this in almost a whisper, a little hurt and embarrassed by how he just treated me. Kal gets up out of his chair and walks away from me, his large feet stomping on the ground. Whenever I have comforted someone who had just been bullied, they didn't really react like that to me. They never really acted angry toward me. My heart jumps a little when I realize why he might be different from the others. All the other people I tried to help were girls. Guys and girls usually react differently to things. When I would try to comfort the girls, they were always very sad and would either talk a lot or not at all about what happened. Kal acted angry, I'm guessing he did that to help him hide his embarrassment and pain. I wonder why girls and guys react differently. I don't have the chance to think this over since Luis rests his hand on my shoulder and gives me a soft smile.

"It's okay Colomba, not everyone wants to be helped." I smile up at Luis, but even I can tell that it isn't very sincere.

"Thanks Luis, I just hate seeing that happen to him. I just wanted to help him feel better." Luis chuckles.

"Well, sometimes we guys don't want to show our feelings, we're too manly for that." He says this in a teasing tone that makes me giggle.

"Oh really?" Luis smiles at me playfully.

"What, do you think that I'm not manly?" I laugh, my unhappiness from what happened with Kal is almost forgotten.

"Maybe." Luis opens his mouth in pretend shock.

"Your words hurt me Madam." I smile at him.

"I thought that manly men didn't show their feelings, or were you lying to me?" I tease him sarcastically.

"Well only the manliest of men can reveal their feelings." He replies with just as much sarcasm as me.

"I'll keep that in mind. C'mon, let's finish getting everything ready. We have a lot of work to do before everyone starts showing up for the game." He nods at me with his soft, gentle smile as he starts helping me get some paper plates and other stuff ready for the sale. As I am fiddling with some plastic forks, I glance over to see that Kal is standing near the teacher's desk while two girls are obviously talking about him, and not in a nice way. They keep glancing at him as they whisper to each other, giggling coldly as they do so. Kal has definitely noticed this since I see his face grow red in embarrassment and his eyes flash with fury. His hands that were holding some extra plastic forks are gripping them so tightly that I'm concerned that he's going to snap them in half. I look away from him because I know that if I keep watching then I will either want to confront those girls about talking about him like that or try to comfort Kal again, which I know will not end well either way.

My smile fades as I keep preparing. All the joy I had felt about doing this bake sale is now gone since I know that a guy is being hurt for no good reason and he doesn't even want my help. I can only sit back and watch as the others laugh and pick on him just because he is bigger than them.

Chapter Twelve
Luis-
A Hurt
Soldier

As Colomba and I start setting up the paper plates and plastic forks, I glance up at her to see that she is staring at something across the room with a very sad look in her aquamarine eyes. I follow her gaze to see that she is looking at Kal. He is angrily doing his job while some girls are giggling in that familiar way that many girls have giggled at me before. I have had this happen many times, they are laughing at him and not trying very hard to hide it.

Kal doesn't even finish his job before he angrily storms out of the room, his huge feet making slapping sounds on the floor as he stomps out the door. This just makes the girls who had been giggling burst into laughter as soon as he is out of the room. I know that I'm a guy, and guys shouldn't hit girls, but man do I want to hit them. Why are they laughing at the poor guy? He wasn't even doing anything to them and during the two meetings we've had for this bake sale, I don't think I've even seen Kal talk to them once.

Looking at Colomba again, she is staring down at the paper plates she has been setting up, from her hunched shoulders and lowered head I can tell that she is upset by what just happened to Kal. I'm about to say something to try and comfort her when she looks up at me and speaks.

"Hey Luis, I'll be right back." She gets up and walks out the door. A sudden thought occurs to me and I get worried. Is she going to try and comfort Kal again? If she is then he's going to get mad at her again. I follow after her, but I have nothing to worry about when it comes to Kal being mean to Colomba. Colomba is just slowly walking down the hall with her head down, clearly still upset. I want to go over there and say something to her, but I know that it won't do anything for her. She feels bad since Kal is in pain and she can't do anything to help him. Colomba is the kind of person who feels everyone's pain, and not being able to help a person in pain is probably one of the worst things she can feel.

I smile to myself as the idea suddenly comes into my head. She may not be able to help him, but I can. I chuckle softly as I think that maybe now is the time for the Crow to make a comeback. I won't let Colomba feel as if Kal isn't getting the respect he deserves as a human being. I can give him that easily.

I give Colomba one last glance as she slowly walks down the hall before I head off to the boy's bathroom. I quickly make sure that nobody is inside before I lock the door and place my hand on the

Crow Medal. Shadow appears on the sink faucet, her dark eyes looking at me with the calm, patient look she gets whenever she knows I'm about to transform someone and knows that there is no way she can convince me to stop.

"Hello Master, I'm guessing that you're going to transform that boy Kal." I only have to nod at her and she knows what to do. I smile as she flies off the faucet and swoops low toward my feet. Her dark wings move faster as she circles around me. I keep smiling as I close my eyes and open them a moment later to look at myself in the mirror and see the Crow looking back at me. I order Shadow to find Kal and I close my eyes again as I see the world through her eyes.

She flies quickly through the hallways as a shadow. She doesn't have any trouble finding him, she could sense his misery. Kal is walking down the hall, his huge body seems to move like a massive lumbering bear. His ginormous belly seems to jiggle with each step his large feet take. Those feet drag across the floor in his sadness, like a snowplow scraping across the street. I smile as I think about how I'm going to be giving him something to pick his feet up for.

Shadow soars right through his back and it takes her a moment to navigate through his massive body to find his heart. When she does get there, I don't waste a moment as I announce myself to him.

Hello Kal. He doesn't even bother to look around to see where the voice is coming from.

"Go away!" He growls this at the empty hallway, and I can't help but chuckle in his mind.

I can't really "go away" Kal, I am in your mind. This catches Kal's attention. He looks around, expecting to find some weird person trying to play a strange prank on him. When he sees that there is nobody there, a spark of realization comes over him.

"You're the Crow." He whispers softly in disbelief.

Yes, I am. I am here so that you can get what you deserve. Respect. The respect that every person deserves to have that everyone has been stealing from you just because you are bigger than them. You deserve to be treated like a human being despite your size. Do you want to be respected? I can give you that. I can even give you something better than respect, I can make them fear you. With fear, you not only have their respect, but you also have power over them. After all the things they have done to you, don't you think that they deserve to have you over them? Don't you deserve to be the one on top for once in your life? I can give you that and more. What do you say? He stops for a moment, thinking about what I just said.

"What can you give me to help me get that?"

Everyone calls you a giant, maybe we should show them what a real giant is. Make them fear you and they will respect you. He smiles as he thinks about what I've said. Kal has always wanted to be respected but has never really felt that people have treated him well. He always feels that people treat him badly since he is so much larger than them and the world doesn't seem to care for people who are bigger. Now he will show them just how wrong they were about him. He chuckles softly as he thinks about what he will do to all of the people who have been hurting him for so long.

"Alright Crow, show me what you've got, and I'll do whatever you say." I chuckle back.

Good choice. When the last word echoes through his head, I let Shadow invade the rest of his body. His heart and mind easily fall to me and I let my power flow through him. Kal starts to laugh out loud as he watches his body begin to morph in front of his eyes. I look through his eyes as his watches his shadow on the row of lockers grow larger and larger while he just keeps laughing, and I laugh right along with him.

Chapter Thirteen
Colomba-
The Giant

People are starting to come into the school for the game, but I am still sitting in a desk and reading a book in the classroom where we had the meeting. I had come in a moment ago after walking in the hallway for a bit to see that Kal was still gone and Luis had run off somewhere. He is probably helping somebody with setting up the bake sale so I'm sure he's fine. It is someone else's turn to watch the bake sale table, so I am waiting for my turn after the game. I could be out there in the gym with everyone else as they wait for the game to start, but I am too upset by what happened with Kal to want to join in the fun. I hope Kal is okay, he seemed so sad and angry by what has been happening to him recently. I really wish that he would have let me try to help him, but I guess Luis is right, some guys don't want to be comforted. I guess it makes them feel less manly having a girl comfort them or something. I don't know, guys are weird.

As I read through my book, I hear something that makes me stop. A sudden booming sound, like thunder from a distance, seems to echo in my ears. I glance around the room, but there is nobody else around me. Am I imagining this? The sound keeps going in a slow but steady rhythm. I glance over to the teacher's desk where she has a plastic vase full of flowers. The petals of the flowers are quivering whenever the thundering sound echoes, and the water at the bottom of the vase is rippling as if something big is coming. The thundering sound seems to be getting closer and closer and I feel my body tense in fear.

Running out of the classroom, I head straight for the gym, terrified that something is happening to everyone in there. When I rush through the doors to the gym, the stands are packed, and everyone is cheering as the home team runs onto the basketball court. Alex leads the team, his muscular arms raised in the air, urging everyone to scream louder for him, which everyone gladly does. The team runs around the basketball court, trying to excite everyone even though everyone is already excited. I try to scream to get everyone's attention, to tell them that something is wrong, but my voice is drowned out by the roar of the cheering. I scream until my throat hurts, but still nobody hears me. I glance around the gym, hoping to find a way to make everyone pay attention when I warn them, but thankfully I don't have to do that, the universe just takes care of that for me.

As the cheering starts to die down when the opposing team comes onto the court, that's when the people in the crowd start to notice that things aren't right. Everyone looks up and around, trying to see what is going on, trying to understand where that sound is coming from. The strange pounding seems to get louder and louder while the gym gets more and more silent as we all wait in terror and curiosity for what we know will happen.

I notice that as the thundering sound gets louder, some popcorn that had dropped on the ground is quivering, as if it is shaking with fear. My heart pounds in my chest in terror. Something is coming, something big. When the booming becomes so intense that I can feel the ground trembling, it suddenly stops. Everyone in the gym looks at each other, trying to understand what happened, but nobody has an answer. Just as quickly as the silence started, it is broken as a horrible tearing sound fills the room, forcing me to cover my ears. It sounds like metal being ripped apart by an incredibly powerful force.

I glance up in my fear to see that the ceiling is getting lifted up and ripped apart from the rest of the building. I quickly get under the stands as pieces of the ceiling start to crumble and rain down to the ground. Everyone follows my example and gets to the safety beneath the stands. I look up to see something that makes me scream in horror, I see what is making the ceiling fall apart. What looks like massive human hands are lifting the ceiling up into the sky to reveal a human being who is taller than the school. I have to look straight up to see the head of this massive person. He looks as if he is five stories tall. I can see several birds flying past his head. I have to squint my eyes to try and look at this giant person's face. Some clouds are slightly covering his hair, but I can clearly see who I am looking at, and my heart breaks when I recognize them.

"Oh no, not you Kal." I whisper to myself while everyone else in the room screams and starts to scatter in panic. When Kal sees how afraid everyone is of him, he releases a huge laugh that echoes through the area, louder than a firework exploding in the sky.

As I stare up in terror at Kal, my horror only grows when I see that he is not alone. A dark shape is flying close to his head. Large black wings come from the creature's back that carry it on the wind. I squint my eyes in the bright light of the setting sun to try and get a better look at it as the creature perches on Kal's shoulder like a strange bird. My heart skips a beat when I recognize that creature, it's the Crow.

I can feel the Crow's eyes burning into my soul as he glares down at all of us. I can't really tell since he is up so high, but I think he is smiling down at all of us, happy to see all of our fear. My hands are shaking at my side in either fear or anger, I'm not really sure which.

What is he doing here? I haven't seen him since he saved me from those fallen rocks when the Sprinter was running around the school almost a year ago. Why did he decide to come back now? I don't get to think about this for very long before Kal takes my attention again. He laughs at the sight of everyone's fear and the sound of it is so loud that I have to cover my ears again. The laughter echoes through the area and birds scatter in the air in terror at this strange danger.

"Students of Drew's Hollow High!" Even with my hands over my ears I can still clearly hear what Kal is shouting at everyone. I wince at the sound of his voice, if he keeps yelling at everyone like this then he is going to break my eardrums. "You are all now under the control of the Crow and me, the Giant!" With that said, he takes the ceiling he had ripped off the building and tears it apart into four pieces. My spine tingles at the horrible sound it makes. It is so loud and painful that I drop to my knees with my hands over my ears. Everyone scatters around me in their panic. They all rush toward the doors, but as soon as they open them, they are greeted to the sight of what seems like an endless amount of the Crow's shadow dogs guarding the doors. The dogs growl and snarl at the crowd and everyone immediately closes the doors in fear. Everyone scrambles around the room, trying to find another exit, but each one seems to be blocked by the shadow dogs.

When he is done ripping the ceiling apart, I watch as he slams the pieces into the ground in the middle of the basketball court. The ground shakes so badly from the force that I am knocked off balance and I fall to the floor. From my position, I can see that the Giant has placed the pieces standing upright in a box shape. What on earth is that for? Why did he do that? He answers my question almost immediately. Using his massive hands, he grabs a handful of people who had been trying to run away. They scream and squirm in his grip, but they cannot escape his grasp. He lifts them up, and then places them within the box he created. I gasp in shock. He has made a cage for everyone.

I need to transform into Silver Dove, and I need to do it now. First though, I need a place to transform where nobody will see me. Watching the Giant, I wait until he has his attention directed on the basketball team, trying to grab all of them in his car sized hands, before I rush out from under the stands to try and make it out of the gym. I hear the team screaming in terror as I move as fast as my legs will carry me, but it is not fast enough.

I almost make it to the doors to the girl's locker room when a huge hand blocks my way and then snatches me into its grasp and lifts me high into the air. As the Giant lifts me up, a sudden and strange thought rushes through my mind. I hope nobody is looking up my dress right now with me high in the air like this.

The Giant lifts me up until he has me right in front of his face. Small clouds float past me, but I don't even bother to look at them. My eyes are glued to the Giant. I don't scream, I know that there is no point. Glancing over to the Crow, who is standing on the Giant's shoulder like a parrot on a pirate's shoulder, I feel my body quiver as I feel his eyes on me. He is staring at me so intensely that I instantly look away in fear. I feel like a coward, but I don't want to look at him. He seems to give off this very dark feeling, and it frightens me.

"Be gentle with this one Giant," the Crow says in his deep, menacing voice. "She is a good girl who has never hurt anybody." The Giant nods at him, not taking his eyes off me.

"I know." The Giant whispers this, but since I am so close to his giant head, it sounds like he is yelling at me. "She has always been kind to me."

The Giant slowly and gently sets me down on the ground inside the little cage that he has made and all the people he has already captured run as far away from his hand as possible as he does so. As soon as his hand disappears from the cage and the Giant goes off to find some more people to capture, the people in the cage with me relax a little bit now that his attention is away from us. What is he planning on doing with all the people he has in this cage? I can't think of an answer, and I don't think I want to know.

My thoughts are interrupted by Alex. His basketball jersey is drenched in sweat even though they didn't even have a chance to play yet. Is he sweating that much in his fear? Gross. I wouldn't be surprised if the answer is yes, his eyes are wide, and his entire body is tense. He runs over and kneels down beside me, his wide eyes looking into mine.

"Colomba, are you okay!?" He quickly wraps me up in his arms, holding me tight to his chest. I gently push away from him, trying not to be rude considering he was just being nice to me.

"I'm okay Alex, really. You don't have to worry about me. The Giant didn't want to hurt me since I was nice to him before the Crow did all this. What's going on in here?" I look around the caged in area and everyone is either huddled on the ground crying or pacing around the place like an animal in a cage. Alex scoffs at everyone when he looks at them even though I can tell that he's just as scared as the rest of them.

"They're just being chickens. Don't you worry though, I'm here to protect you from that giant thing." He pulls me in close again while I roll my eyes. So not only do I need to find a way out of here so that I can transform, but I also need to do it so that nobody else can see me and follow me out of the cage and get the Giant's attention, and I also need to get away from Alex. This is not going to be fun.

Chapter Fourteen
Luis-
Watching the
Chaos

I stand on the Giant's shoulder, watching the people run wildly around the basketball court as they try to find a place to escape. They are such fools. My shadow dogs are guarding every exit, they have no way of getting out. The Giant swings his massive hands down and scoops up more people and places them in the cage he made with parts of the ceiling. I have no idea what he plans on doing with all the people in the cage, and I don't think he knows either, but I don't let that bother me. I'm too busy enjoying the scene in front of me. Everyone is so terrified of my creation, and Silver Dove is nowhere to be found. This is just perfect; she must have not been attending the game tonight. I guess she doesn't have the superpower of being everywhere at once, too bad for her. I suppose I will finally be winning this round.

The Giant had placed Colomba in the cage just a moment ago, and a feeling of guilt hangs in my stomach like a rock. I didn't want him to put her in there with the rest of those people, but I couldn't let her go either or else people would get suspicious or Colomba might figure out that I may know her and that might lead her to suspect that her old friend Luis is the Crow. She has suspected me before, and I don't want her to do that again. Convincing her that I wasn't the Crow was hard enough the first time, I don't think I could figure out a way to convince her a second time.

Looking far down at the ground, I watch Colomba as another figure comes up close to her, much too close. With the basketball jersey on, even from this far up, it's easy for me to see that it's Alex trying to comfort her. My blood starts to boil in my veins until I see her gently push him away to have some space. Dang, even in a scary situation like this, she still won't let him near her. Seeing that just puts a smile on my face, but what I also see makes me feel very nervous and confused. Everyone in the cage is acting very scared, pacing around the cage and crying their eyes out, but not Colomba. She is so calm that it almost looks like she's about to go on a pleasant stroll through the park instead of being trapped by a giant in a cage with a bunch of other people. This strange look on her face drives me nuts with curiosity.

I leap off the Giant's shoulder and open my wings out wide so that I can fly down closer to the top of the cage. I land on top of one of the chunks of ceiling that he used to create the cage and everyone inside quickly moves to the opposite side of the cage from me. They all cower close together, like lambs facing a hungry wolf. Everyone does this, everyone except Colomba. She had remained where she was, kneeling on the ground near the center of the cage. Colomba is staring right at me, well not really staring, more like glaring at me. She is glaring at me as if she is just a bit angry with me, like I have only annoyed her with everything I have done tonight. The two of us don't break eye contact for what feels like ages. I look at her with, what I'm hoping, looks like a kind, reassuring face, but she just continues to glare at me. I'm the one who breaks our gaze, kind of intimidated by her intense glare.

Wow, the last time I had shown up as the Crow in front of her, she was absolutely terrified of me, but now she's glaring at me as if I'm a small child that is irritating her. I have seen Colomba do some pretty impressive stuff with martial arts, but I've never been scared of her, not until she glared at me like that. The look she gave me was something I have never seen before when I am the Crow. It was a look with absolutely no fear even in the presence of what could be danger. In her eyes, I saw pure hatred. It not only scared me, but also broke my heart to see her looking at me with that much hate. Even with my face turned away from her, I can still feel her glare burning me on the side of my face.

I feel like a complete wimp, but I open up my wings and fly away so that I can get away from those burning eyes of hers. From the corner of my eye, I can see that as soon as I left my perch on top of the cage, everyone else inside stopped cowering on the opposite side of the cage and started spreading out again to give each other some room, but Colomba still stayed in her position, never letting that glare leave me.

My wings take me high into the air and I stop when I am close to the same height as the Giant's head. I stay in one place, my wings flapping gently as I glance below me to watch the Giant continue on with his work. I try to make myself enjoy this victory, but I can't. I can't enjoy this because I can still feel that dark glare burning straight into my soul.

Chapter Fifteen
Colomba-
Escape

Everyone is acting like a bunch of crazy people in the cage the Giant has made. Several people are crying around me, tears flowing down their faces like water going down a waterfall. While they are all acting like a bunch of looneys, I'm just sitting on the ground without any fear. With me so calm while everyone is going nuts, I'm almost like the eye of a storm. I can't feel any fear right now, I'm too angry. I can't believe I got captured by one of the Crow's little slaves. This is just embarrassing. I mean, I'm Silver Dove. I shouldn't be getting captured, I should be stopping him right now but I can't because I am stuck in this cage with a bunch of other people who I can't transform in front of. What's making it worse is that Alex is trying to hang around me, trying to hold me, to comfort me, and tell me that everything is going to be alright. I already know that everything will be alright though, if he would just go away so I can have some peace and quiet so I can figure out what I'm going to do. I keep telling him that I'm alright, but he won't listen. I feel myself groan softly as Alex asks me for the millionth time if I'm alright.

"Yes Alex, I'm fine." I try to keep the growl out of my voice, but with how angry I am right now that's really hard.

"What can I do to make you feel better?" He leers at me as he says this, making my skin crawl.

"You don't have to do anything for me Alex, I swear I'm fine." I glance over to see that the other members of the basketball team are huddled together, chatting worriedly as they look up at the Giant. It's so strange to see those guys like this. Whenever it's a normal day at school, they strut down the halls like they are so tough, but here they are quivering like leaves in the wind in their fear. Well, I guess you don't really know how tough you are until you are in a tough situation. When I look at them though, it gives me a great idea. "I may not need anything Alex, but it looks like your team does." Alex glances over at them for the first time since I was put in this cage.

"Oh they're big boys, they can take care of themselves. It's you that I'm worried about." He leers at me again and I have to look away from him to prevent myself from rolling my eyes at how cheesy he sounded. I rest my hand on top of his, trying to convince him.

"They need you more than I do Alex, they need their team captain to help them figure out what to do." It doesn't look like he's completely convinced so I give his hand a little squeeze. "It would mean a lot to me if you helped them." I give him my best puppy dog eye look and he melts. Alex smiles at me warmly.

"Alright Beautiful, I'll do it." He stands up and takes a few steps toward his team members before he turns back to face me. "I'll be back for you though, so wait for me girl." It takes all my strength to not puke at how much he sounds like a stupid action movie, but I manage to smile back at him.

"I'll be right here." He turns back and starts yelling at his team members to shape up and stop acting like "a bunch of little girls". As soon as he had his back turned, I was running toward the edge of the cage. As if I would wait for him, I need to find a way to escape, this "little girl" needs to save the day.

While everyone is still freaking out, I start examining every inch of the pieces of ceiling used to make this cage. The twisted metal and pieces of rock seem to have no way of getting through to the other side. My eyes scan each scrap of debris to see if I can easily move it or if there is a way out behind it. I examine two of the four walls before I find something promising. In one of the corners, the Giant didn't put the two ceiling pieces together quite right. Near the ground there is a small opening, when I look at it, I can tell that probably nobody can fit through it since it is so small. Nobody except me that is. I am smaller than practically everyone else my age, something that has always bothered me since everyone thinks that I am weak because of it. Well, I guess if being smaller had to be useful at least one time in my life, it might as well be now.

I look into the hole in the cage to see that it may not be safe to go through. I can see light coming from the other side, but there are some things that may cause some problems on the way out. The edge of the tunnel is jagged, with pieces of rock and metal sticking out at every angle. It almost looks like the mouth of a monster that's just waiting for me to crawl in so that it can eat me. For the first time since being put in this strange cage, I actually feel afraid. If I go through that hole, I could tear myself apart while trying. I could get really hurt or possibly die. The hole could collapse around me, leaving me buried under all that debris. I feel myself back away from the hole, unsure of what to do. Am I going to risk it and try to go through there and possibly die, or will I stay in here and let the Crow and the Giant win? I look around me at the other trapped people, in their eyes I can see that they share my fear. They are scared that the Giant or the Crow will do something terrible to them and, just like me, they're scared that they may die.

I lower my head, feeling ashamed of myself. What am I doing? I am supposed to be the hero here, not a sniveling coward. I am Silver Dove, I am the one that everyone here is waiting for to save the day. I can't let myself be afraid now. I can't let myself be beaten before I have even started the battle. I look back at the hole in the wall and hold back my fear as I get down on my stomach and start sliding through the hole.

I try to keep my body as close to the ground as possible so that I won't scratch myself on the pointed rocks and sharp pieces of broken metal only an inch or so above me. My body slides across the floor so slowly I feel like a worm crawling on the ground. Using my hands to drag myself, I also use them to push small rocks and other debris out of my way so that they won't scratch my stomach as I slide on the floor. I watch the light at the end of the tunnel as I make my way through, but it feels as if I am moving slower than a snail. As I try and pull myself forward a little farther, I hear a horrific tearing sound and I look back to see that a piece of metal had ripped a jagged gash down my dress, just missing my skin by a miracle. I take in a shaky breath as I count my blessings before I continue on my strange journey toward the end of the tunnel.

It feels like hours have passed, when it was probably only a few minutes, before I make it to the exit. I want to rush out and get away from all this craziness, but I know that if I do that then I will just get swiped up by the Giant and he will just put me back in the cage and I'll have to go through that creepy, dangerous tunnel again. I have to be more careful with this. Slowly, I peek my head out of the tunnel and look straight up at the Giant before quickly moving back in the tunnel. My heart is pounding in my chest, he was looking this way. Did he see me? I can hear my deep breathing echoing in the tunnel as the fear makes my head pound and I feel a headache forming already.

I take in a few deep breaths before I look out again to see that the Giant apparently didn't notice me since he is scanning the area, looking for more people to catch. From where I am, I can see a teenage girl hiding behind the basketball scoreboard that had fallen down during all the chaos. She is shivering so much in her fear that she almost looks like she's dying of cold. She peeks out from behind the scoreboard to look at the Giant and as soon as his back is turned, she bolts out from behind there to try and make a break for the door. The Giant must have heard her or something since he turns his head around and spots her instantly. His massive hand grabs her just as her hand touched the door. The Giant lifts her into the air and as I hear her start to scream, I finally recognize who she is, it's Angela. I stare up in horror, unsure of what is going to happen. Angela was cruel to him just the other day and I doubt that he's gotten over it since then, what is he going to do to her?

The Giant holds her right in front of his face, smiling coldly at her as he chuckles so loudly that it feels like my entire world is shaking and I'm scared that the tunnel might cave in around me from the force. I'm afraid to see what happens next, but I also can't look away, I'm too curious to see what will happen. Even from here I can hear Angela begging the Giant to let her go, that she didn't mean what she said the other day, and that she would love to go out on a date with him. It's obvious to both me and the Giant that she is lying, so he just smirks at her before he brings her back down. He surprises me by not putting her in the cage along with everyone else, he has something special in mind for her. The Giant carefully places her butt first into the basketball goal. Her weight makes her sink down so that, no matter how hard she squirms, she can't get her butt out of the goal and she is trapped.

As all of this is going on, the Crow is watching, flying in the air with an evil grin appearing underneath his mask. He looks like he is having the time of his life watching the Giant be mean to Angela. Honestly, it is kind of funny seeing Angela stuck in the basketball hoop, but it doesn't mean he should let this happen. I just want to whack that obnoxious smirk off his face, he wouldn't be smiling like that for very long if I punched in the face with my super strength… Okay I probably shouldn't do that. I don't think he has invincibility like me, and I don't want to punch his face just for it to cave in like in those old cartoons. That would be super gross and creepy, also I'm pretty sure that not even he could recover from that. I may not like the guy, but I don't want to kill him. I shiver at the thought that if he was in my shoes, he may try to kill me.

I don't have time to think about this anymore though since both the Giant and the Crow turn away to focus on some other people across the broken remains of the gym that they want to capture too. This is my chance. I rush out of the tunnel and quickly hide in between some broken pieces of the ceiling that had crashed down near the girl's locker room. It is quiet and secluded here. I look around myself to see that there is nobody around me. I shudder when I realize that there may be nobody else left for the Giant to capture and then he will finally do what he has been planning on doing with those people in the cage, whatever that is.

I place my hand over my Dove Pin, take a deep breath, and say the magic words, "Peaceful warrior." I close my eyes as I feel the change come over me. I feel my hands close into fists. This is it, I have no idea how I'm going to do this, but I have to try something. As soon as I can feel that the transformation is over, I open my eyes and my wings, ready to fight for my life, as well as for the lives of everyone in that cage.

Chapter Sixteen
Luis-
A Missing
Girl, An
Unwanted Girl

I watch with a smile on my face as the Giant lifts up the final people who had been in the hiding in the gym and places them in the cage he created. The cage is practically full now since there had been so many people at the game. Now that the last person has been captured, it's time for part two of the plan, what part two is I have no idea. I still have no idea why the Giant placed everyone in this cage or what he wants to do with them. Maybe since he's a giant he will grind their bones to make his bread or something… Okay I really hope not, that sounds really gross.

As the Giant looks down at all the people he trapped, looking very pleased with himself, I look down too feeling very proud as well as very confused. I'm proud that the Giant has gotten this far, but I'm also surprised that he's gotten this far too. I know that news must have traveled all over town by now about what has happened here, I can even hear the police cars in the school parking lot that are being held back by my army of shadow dogs. If everybody in town knows about this, then where is Silver Dove? None of my other soldiers have ever made it this far, why hasn't anything happened to ruin it yet? I suddenly feel angry with myself and I push those thoughts out of my head. I am finally winning; I shouldn't let myself think like that. I should enjoy this moment.

As I look through the crowd of people in the cage though, I find the answer to my question. I have found something to ruin this moment. My eyes scan the crowd in the cage, but one person is missing, the most important person. Where is Colomba? I look through the crowd several more times, but she is still missing. Where did she go? How did she get out? My stomach lurches inside me as I start to worry. Is she alright? Did she get hurt when trying to escape? If she's not in there, and she doesn't seem to be in the gym either, where could she be? I mean my shadow dogs are guarding the doors so she can't escape, but she doesn't seem to be anywhere in the gym, so where could she possible be?!

I look up at the Giant and the idiot obviously hasn't figured out that she is gone yet. I growl softly to myself as I fly straight into the air and stop right next to his ear. I cup my hands around my mouth to make sure that I am as loud as possible, just to hurt his ears.

"Giant!!" He is so surprised by my sudden yell that he actually stumbles back a bit and steps on the bleachers, turning them into a splintered mess of wood.

"What? What is it?" He asks me with panic shining in his massive eyes the size of bowling balls.

"Why did I give powers to such a stupid kid like you?! Haven't you noticed that one of your prisoners is missing?!" The Giant's eyes just seem to get bigger as he stares at me in complete shock. His head quickly snaps down to look at the cage, after a moment he looks very confused.

"Who's missing?" I slap his ear with my wing in my frustration, which makes him stumble back again, wrecking even more of the bleachers.

"Colomba is missing! You know, the one you said had been kind to you!" He opens his mouth slightly in surprise and horror when he sees how angry I am. He stammers for a moment before he can actually get a sentence out.

"I- I'm sorry Crow, I really am. I didn't mean to-" I interrupt him by slapping him across the nose with my wing.

"Don't give me that "I'm sorry" junk! Find her or I will take away your powers!" He nods his head, looking very serious. My body instantly becomes tense at the sight of that, and I quickly add more to make sure he doesn't mess up. "And remember what you said earlier about her, she is a nice person, so don't you dare hurt her!" I fly closer to his eyes so that he can see my glare more clearly. "If you do hurt her, you have me to deal with. Don't disappoint me again!" With how big he is, it is easy to see that he is quivering in terror.

"Of course Crow. I won't let you down, I promise." I tighten my hands into fists, and I let my glare grow even darker.

"You better. If you fail me, I will make sure that your existence is shorter than you hoped." The Giant nods as pure terror lights up his eyes. It is beautiful to see. Of course, I would never hurt him like that, but I'm not going to let him know that, having him fear me makes my power over him so much stronger. I start scanning the area along with him, searching for any sign of Colomba. The Giant is looking for her out of fear of me, but I'm looking because I fear for her. She could be hurt somewhere for all I know. As I glance around the gym, a sudden thought comes into my mind and won't leave. Colomba is a very kind and helpful person, so why didn't she help the other people in the cage get out? If she found a way out, she would have led everyone to safety when the Giant and I were distracted. This doesn't make any sense. My head swivels on my neck, my search gets more frantic as I get more and more worried with each passing second. I make sure to pass a message through my mind to my shadow dogs to remind them that they should never harm Colomba, as I have told them a million times before, but in my mind, I know that they haven't seen Colomba all night. They are just as clueless about where she is as I am. This only makes me feel ten times worse.

One small thing makes me feel a bit better though. Angela is still kicking and squirming, trying to get herself out of the basketball hoop. Her blonde hair is whipping around her face as she keeps twisting and turning in the hoop. Even though I am worried about Colomba, it still makes me feel good to see Angela like this. It's nice to have that snobby girl be put in her place.

I fly over to her, only stopping when I am about five feet in front of her. She instantly stops moving and looks at me with terror. With all the movement she was doing a second ago, her usually perfectly styled hair is hanging in her face and sticking out at odd angles. She almost looks like her hair was attacked by a vacuum or something. The basketball net twitches slightly as she shivers in her fear. I stay silent, just looking at her intensely for another minute just to make her more anxious about what I plan on doing. Just from looking into her eyes, I can tell that she thinks that I might try to hurt her, or worse.

After I've let her stew in her fear, I make it worse. I chuckle darkly, making her already large eyes grow wider and I watch her entire body tense in horror. Maybe I should join the theatre club or something, apparently I could play a really good bad guy considering how scared I make people as the Crow. If only I could make people this afraid of me without the mask. Maybe one day I will be able to do that, one day people will fear and respect me as just Luis and not just as the Crow.

My thoughts are interrupted as I hear a strange sound to the side of me, it almost sounds as if something is moving really fast through the air. I don't have time to glance over to my side before something hits me so hard that I fly through the air and crash down so hard on the ground that a wave of pain comes over me. I had landed on my side and my shoulder had gone numb as soon as I hit the ground. Fear is now rushing through me as I lay on the ground, terrified that I may have broken my shoulder.

In my agony, I look up to see a figure flying above me, their snowy white wings flapping gently as they glare down at me. Even in my pain, I lift myself up into a sitting position to glare back at my enemy, Silver Dove.

"Giant! Come over here you massive idiot! Can't you see that we have an unwelcome visitor!" The Giant stops his frantic search to glance over and see that Silver Dove has finally arrived. Silver Dove doesn't even give him a chance to react though before she goes into action. She soars through the air straight toward me and before I'm able to get back up to fly away from her, she had grabbed me underneath my arms and is now flying straight up into the air with me in her grasp. She flies so high, so quickly that she and I are now out of the Giant's grasp and he can no longer help me. Silver Dove holds me up so that the two of us are now face to face.

"Why are you doing this Crow? Why are you here?" She growls this in a menacing tone that most people would find intimidating, but I just laugh at her.

"What? Don't tell me that you are upset to see your old friend." Her nose crinkles in disgust and her eyes, that are slightly hidden by her mask, clearly show her fury.

"I offered to be your friend once and you didn't accept me then, and I'm not going to accept you now if you keep this up. I haven't heard of you showing up in person since the incident with the Sprinter, so *why* are you here now?" I laugh in her face, not answering her question. The truth is that I don't really have an answer to her question. Why did I show up in person this time? Maybe I just wanted to see the mayhem with my own eyes, or maybe I just wanted to remind everyone that I'm still here. Either way, I'm here now and I'm finally face to face with Silver Dove. She is glaring at me now with so much fury that I'm afraid she might punch me in the face with her super strength.

"I'm just here to help my soldier Silver Dove, someone around here has to defend the people who can't defend themselves. We can't all be like you who defends all the people who are hurting everyone else." I can feel her hands tighten on me and I'm worried that I went too far, I'm going to get beaten up any second.

"Don't be so smug Crow. How can you think that all this destruction is a good idea? Your medal must have done something to your brain to make you go nuts! There's no other way to explain how you can believe something so crazy unless you are just stupid. Are you that stupid?" Now it is my turn to feel angry.

"Maybe I am seeing sense and you're the stupid one for not realizing the truth." She takes a deep breath, probably trying to control herself so that she doesn't punch me. I keep talking, really wanting to make her see my side. "Aren't you tired of doing this same pattern? People are mean to someone, I show up and transform that someone, you fight that person, they surrender and give up those powers, and then everything returns to normal with everyone being cruel to each other again. Can't you see that you're only making things worse? You're just letting these people think that they can get away with it, that they can be mean to others without anything bad happening to them. I'm just teaching them a lesson so that maybe one day things can be better for everyone. Maybe you can help with that so that nobody gets hurt again." As I was talking, her expression had changed slightly. She is no longer mad, she is looking at me with curiosity, as if she is really thinking about what I am saying. My heart skips a beat when I realize that she might actually change her mind, she might actually join me. That hope is quickly shattered though when that thoughtful expression changes instantly back into fury.

"Okay then, my earlier question has been answered. You *are* just that stupid." My anger overcomes me and I swing my wing toward her and it hits her right across the face. She lets go of me in her surprise and I don't waste a second, I fly downward as fast as I can. It doesn't take long for Silver Dove to recover before she is flying after me, just like I want her to. I swoop down right in front of the face of the Giant, and Silver Dove doesn't realize my plan before it is too late. She tries to turn and go the opposite way, but the Giant can reach her now. I smile coldly as the Giant starts swinging his arms right at her. I hear myself chuckle as I think, let the fun begin.

Chapter Seventeen
Colomba-
A Giant Boy,
A Little Dove

I fly through the air, wanting to get to the Crow who is only a few yards away from me, but the Giant is keeping me away from my goal. My wings are flapping as hard as they can, trying to not get hit by his huge hands as they swing out at me wildly. The Giant uses his massive hand to try and swat me out of the air like a bug. I suddenly have more sympathy for bugs. I dodge his hand again as it flies through the air, but this time he was faster than I expected, and he finally gets one good swing in. I don't even have time to turn my head to look at the hand coming toward me. When his hand hits me it feels like I've been hit by a bus. My body flies through the air and I don't have time to catch myself with my wings to return to the fight before I crash through the wall of the gym and then smash through the next wall and the next, until I smash into the ground with so much force that my body creates a small crater in the floor of the wood shop.

I moan softly. I would have thought that he would take it easy on me since I'm a girl and a nice guy like Kal isn't somebody you would expect to hit a girl. Apparently, when you have superpowers politeness doesn't really matter. Well, I try to be polite at least, apparently Kal doesn't think the same way.

I pick myself up and shake out my wings, rubble from the wall and wood shavings from the wood shop fall off the feathers of my wings. I glance back at my wings to see that that jerk has broken some of my feathers. I may not be able to get hurt, but it doesn't mean that my feathers can't get broken. I am so totally going to take this guy down for damaging my beautiful wings.

I take off into the air and enter the gym again through the holes in the walls I created. I fly off to the Giant's side so that he can't see me. As I fly, I raise my fist in front of me so that I can punch him across the face. Even with my super strength, this only makes him stumble a little bit from the impact. He roars in frustration, making the world shake from the strength of his voice. My ears ring and my helmet vibrates. I am dazed by the roar, which gives him the chance to try and swat at me again. I'm prepared this time though. I weave through the air, dodging his massive hands flying toward me. The wind he creates from swinging around his massive hands is so powerful that he almost knocks me off course. It takes all my concentration to keep flying toward him.

Unsheathing my sword, I swipe at one of his hands coming toward me. He releases another roar, but not one of frustration like before, this is one of pain and surprise. He growls and roars in frustration as he uses his other hand to make a fist. He swings this at me too, but now I am more confident. I slash at his oncoming fist with my sword and create a cut on his knuckle. He brings his hand back as he roars again. I would usually feel bad about hurting him like this, but with how big he is and how small my sword is, it probably just feels like a bad papercut to him. He shakes his hand that is now a bit bloody from the cut I gave him.

While he is distracted, I put my sword back in its sheathe. I won't be able to win the fight with him like this, I need to get closer so that I can talk to him. Drops of his blood drip from his hand as I fly only a few yards in front of his face.

"Kal!" He looks up at me in surprise. "Can we talk?" He doesn't say an answer, but he surely shows me what he wants. He swings his hand toward me, trying to swat me again. I swoop down low to avoid it and I realize that I need to get him in a weak position before I try to talk to him again. I glance around, trying to find something that I can use against him. My eye catches sight of something that gives me hope. It's a long thick rope that is usually attached to the ceiling so that people can climb up it to ring a bell. Just something to exercise with in gym class. Since the Giant ripped off the ceiling, the rope is just laying on the ground without any purpose. I smile as I think that I will give it a purpose again, one a lot different than what it is used to.

As the Giant swings his hand at me again, I

swoop down so quickly that I can hear a few of the people in the cage gasp in fear, afraid that I will hit the ground, but I open my wings wide at the last second and fly back up into the air with the rope in my hands. I hear them cheer for me, but I don't pay attention, I have work to do. The Giant doesn't even have a chance to figure out what I am planning before I spring into action.

I fly low to the ground, I go for his shoes first. The rope is easily tied to his shoelaces on one shoe. With that done, I finish the job, flying as fast as possible, I circle around Kal, flying steadily higher. All of this done while still holding the rope tightly, wrapping it securely around his legs. I can see his eyes grow wide when he figures out what I am doing, but it is too late. The rope has now been wrapped tightly several times around his legs and he can no longer balance. His body wobbles and he starts to fall and my heart skips a beat when I see where he is going to land, right on top of the people trapped in the cage. The screaming of terror from the people in the cage powers my flight as I fly faster than I ever have before. I fly right underneath the Giant as he starts to fall and then straight up toward him. When he is just about to slam right into me, I let out a fist and punch him in the face with such force that his body jerks backward and he falls on top of what remains of the bleachers, completely missing the cage.

The cage full of people erupts into cheers, but I keep my eyes on the Giant as he squirms, trying to get himself into a sitting position with his entire lower body tied up. I use this moment of weakness to make my move. Flying straight toward him, I can hear the people cheering again, probably thinking that I'm going to hit him, but I disappoint them. I stop only a few yards from his face, looking him straight in the eyes.

"Kal, you need to talk to me before you make a mistake that you can't fix." I look over at the cage full of people and I feel my heart sinking into my chest and my stomach churn in fear and disgust. "I don't know what you were planning on doing with everyone in the cage, but I can take a guess. *That* is a mistake you can't fix, *don't* go there. You have more in your life than just right now. Right now may be very hard for you, but it doesn't mean that you can hurt these people to make you feel better about yourself." Kal narrows his huge eyes at me in rage.

"Shut up! You're not the boss of me! You don't know anything about me! You're probably one of the people who deserves to be in that cage with the rest of them, you're just hiding it behind that mask of yours and acting so high and mighty!" I sigh at him, feeling completely annoyed and frustrated.

"I'm not hiding anything, I'm just trying to help you not do something that you will regret for the rest of your life. This isn't the way to get what you want and need in this world. Hurting people doesn't get you that. It may make you feel good at the moment, but it will come back to bite you." Kal just shakes his head.

"You're just like them, I can tell. You hate me just like them, so why should I listen to you? You just want me to stop so that I won't hurt your friends in there, you don't care about me at all." I slowly fly away from his face and land on his shoulder. He turns his head to look at me, and I gently rest my hand on his face, trying to show him a little bit of sympathy in this dark moment.

"I could never hate you, you are a very sweet person. You deserve better than how they were treating you, but from the way you are acting now, you may be proving all of those people right." Kal's eyes grow wide at my sudden harsh words. "Kal, you have to see that this won't help you. You say that everyone hates you because you're bigger than them, that they make fun of you for this even though you have done nothing to them. Do you think that doing this will make them like you more?" Kal glances over at the cage that stands only a few feet away from his foot as if thinking about what I just said before the anger returns in a blazing fire in his eyes.

"I don't care if they like me or not! They don't mean anything to me!" I narrow my eyes at him.

"If they don't mean anything to you, then why are you so upset by their words?" He instantly calms down and he looks ashamed of himself. Kal looks down at his tied up feet, looking just like a small child who has been caught doing something naughty. I'm about to say something more when something takes my attention away from Kal.

I hear the hurried fluttering of large wings, I glance around Kal's head to see the Crow flying down onto Kal's other shoulder. The Crow's fists are clenched in fury as he glares at Kal. When Kal sees his rage, he looks back at his shoes, completely terrified by the angry look of his master. I have to hold back a giggle at a strange thought that suddenly flashes through my mind. With me and the Crow perched on his shoulders, it kind of reminds me of those old cartoons where a person has an angel and a demon on their shoulders telling them to do good or bad. If this wasn't such a serious situation, I would have burst out laughing about it.

"Don't listen to her Giant!" The Crow screams on Kal's other shoulder. "She is just trying to trick you so that you will give up your powers and you'll be right back where you were before! Everyone will still be making fun of you and think that you're a loser!" I can see that Kal is starting to get convinced by what the Crow is saying, so I interrupt him before he can say anything else.

"I never thought of you like that Kal!" Kal looks at me with hope in his eyes, as if he's hoping that I'll change his mind about doing all of this. "I saw you as you are, a sweet guy who deserves to be treated with respect. So what if you're bigger than them. We are all made differently, we can't all look alike. If you want to be thinner then you can work on that, but don't do it because those people tell you to. Do it because you want to. Do it because you want to be healthier, so that you can be stronger and do things that you never thought you could do before. No matter how you feel, hurting these people won't help. What you're feeling isn't controlled by them or me, it's controlled by you. If you destroy me, this school, and those people then you'll still be stuck with yourself. We are not the ones controlling how you feel, not even the Crow has that power. You are the only one who has any control over how you feel." The Giant looks as if he is thinking about what I have said, the Crow sees this too and he instantly grows even more furious.

"Don't you even think about it Giant! Don't let her beat you! Don't let her have power over you!" I can see the Crow's face beginning to grow red beneath his mask in his fury. He knows that I am starting to get Kal on my side and he can't stand it.

"Kal wait!" The Giant looks back at me, his huge eyes looking down at me with fear, not knowing what he needs to do. "Think about all of the things he has been saying to you. He has been promising you power, you may have power over these people that you have captured, but he has complete power over you. He has been hanging that over your head ever since he gave you these powers. Even if you defeat me and get revenge on all these people, can you live in fear of the Crow for the rest of your life? 'Cus that's what's going to happen if you keep going. Revenge is a two-edged sword. That means that you might hurt someone else like you want, but revenge will hurt you too. Think about that before you decide what you need to do. Just know this, if you do decide to give up your powers, I will be here to protect you. I have defeated the Crow before, and I can do it again." Kal's face lights up with hope, knowing that he may not have to do what he had been planning, he can get out of making this stupid decision. I smile up at Kal, trying to show him that I am here for him, but a yell of fury comes from Kal's other shoulder. I look around Kal's head to see the Crow shaking with rage.

"I've had enough of this!" The Crow lifts a stiff hand toward me, and a pack of his shadow dogs appear at his side and they follow his silent command. They charge at me with their dark fangs biting at the air and their howls sending a shiver down my spine. I leap off of Kal's shoulder so that he won't get hurt in this fight as I pull out my sword. They all charge at me and I feel my stomach flipping in my stomach in my fear. Taking in a deep breath, I swallow my fear and release a roar as I charge toward the pack, my sword raised.

I slash down at the leader of the pack and it disappears like the shadow it is at the incredible force I put behind that swing. The other shadow dogs don't let the disappearance of their leader slow them down since they just continue charging at me like a herd of bulls. My sword swipes through the air at them, making them disappear too one by one. As my sword swings straight through one of them, I am not fast enough to turn around to notice the one that had been sneaking up behind me. I feel a set of teeth wrap around my leg and I let out a scream of surprise. As Silver Dove, I can't get hurt, but I can still feel the dog as he uses his impressive strength to pull my leg out from under me and I fall to the ground. The other shadow dogs take advantage of my moment of weakness and pounce on me like the predators they are. They try to rip apart my flesh with their monstrous teeth, but they don't get anywhere with my impervious skin getting in their way. I try to fling them off of me, my legs kicking out and one arm swinging my sword while the other swings punches. It doesn't take the dogs long to figure out a solution to that problem. Several of them latch their teeth onto the arm holding my sword and pin it to the ground, preventing me from slashing at them with it. When I try to use my free hand to rip one of them off the pinned arm, a few more shadow dogs come around and use their teeth to pin that arm too. With those arms useless, the other dogs seize their chance. They leap onto my body and pin my legs to the ground so that I can't kick them. I am now stuck under a massive pile of these dogs. The sound of their fangs against the metal of my armor sets my teeth on edge. I want to cover my ears so badly, but I can't, I am helpless. In my fear, I release a scream of horror. With that scream heard, one brave soul shows me mercy.

It feels as if a massive wind has come through the remains of the gym and it is so powerful that about a dozen of the shadow dogs fly off of me, yelping in surprise and pain. The wind comes by again, coming from the other direction, sending even more dogs scattering. With so many of them off me now, I can clearly look above me to see that Kal is using his giant hands to swat the dogs away, sending them flying to hit the walls, dissolving into nothingness as they do so. The Crow is flying around Kal's head as he is doing this while screaming something at Kal that I can't hear over the sound of the shadow dogs all over me, biting at my armor or whimpering as they get thrown off of me by Kal. I may not know what he is screaming, but judging from how angry he looks, they aren't nice words. Tears are falling down Kal's face, dripping off his chin, and plummeting down to the ground like the world's biggest rain drops. Some of the dogs near him run away with their tails between their legs, trying to avoid being hit by the massive tear drops. They splash to the ground as if someone just dumped a bucket of water. When all the dogs have scattered, Kal remains where he is, the tears still falling.

"I'm done!" Kal shouts this, making the shadow dogs whimper at the massive noise. "I'm done! I don't want to do this anymore! I don't want to hurt anybody! I'm sick of this! Just make me myself again! I don't want to live like this!" I smile as I watch Kal's giant body slowly shrink as the Crow glares at him with pure hatred. Kal keeps shrinking until he is the same size as he was before the Crow decided to ruin things. Kal is now standing in the massive puddles that were his tears only moments before, but now much smaller tears are still falling down his face and dripping off his chin to create ripples in those ocean like puddles. He looks up at me through his tear covered eyelashes, the look in his eyes tells me that he expects me to lecture at him like a mom getting mad at their child for being naughty. I don't do that to him though, I just give him a soft smile, showing him that it will be alright.

This peaceful moment between Kal and I is shattered when I hear the fluttering of large wings. I glance over to my side quickly, expecting to be attacked any second, but I am greeted to the sight of the Crow just landing only fifteen feet away from me. The Crow's eyes seem to glow behind his mask in his rage, but I do not feel any fear this time. I step between Kal and the Crow, unsure of what the Crow might do to him in his anger. The Crow glares at me with so much hatred that it is kind of unnerving. I have never seen so much hatred in one person. Pulling out my sword, I point it straight at his face.

"I wouldn't take another step closer if I was you, also you may want to just run away because I'm about to get things back to normal and I don't think all the people you helped trap in that cage are going to be very happy to see you." As if to prove my point, the people in the cage start making a ton of noise, screaming and yelling, demanding that they be let out and making terrible threats toward the Crow. The Crow looks over to the cage for a moment and an instant of fear passes over his face before a smug grin spreads across his lips.

"As if they scare me, they are powerless against me. They will never defeat me, no matter how many there are." I take a few steps closer to him, keeping my sword directed at his face.

"You wouldn't feel so smug if I did release them and I joined their side, now get out of here before I decide whether I should give you a little poke with this or not." I thrust the sword toward him, and I notice that he flinched when I did that. I have to admit that made me feel good to see that fear. His smug grin returns before he speaks again.

"Good bye Silver Dover, I'll see you soon." His head turns ever so slightly so that he can look at Kal with a burning glance. "I hope you get what you deserve for turning your back on someone trying to help you." Without another word, the doors to the gym burst open to reveal all of the shadow dogs he had created earlier to guard the doors. I point my sword at them, but there is no point. The shadow dogs don't pay any attention to me, they just swarm around the Crow until he is lost in the shadows. The dogs writhe and dash around him with such fast movements that they all blur into one huge mass of blackness. As soon as it had started, it was all over. The blackness disappeared along with the Crow, not even leaving a trace of him behind. You know, if I wasn't so annoyed, I would actually be impressed by his dramatic exit. I look around the gym for a second, just to make sure that he really is gone before I turn my attention to Kal. Kal is looking around too, terror lighting up his face.

"It's alright Kal, he is gone." His wandering eyes finally rest on me, becoming instantly calm at my words. "Are you ready to have things go back to normal?" Kal looks over at the cage he had made when he was under the influence of the Crow. "Don't worry Kal, I will keep you safe." He tries to smile at me, but with the fear still on his face it looks more like a grimace. Kal gives me a nod and I understand what he means. Placing my hand over the dove on my chest armor, I say the magic words.

"Bring peace little dove." The dove on my armor flies off and flaps its wings high into the air. When it has gone as high as where the ceiling used to be, I know what is about to happen. I use my wings to shield both me and Kal. A blinding light fills the gym for an instant and then disappears again. I lower my wing to reveal that the gym now looks exactly like it did before the Giant came and ripped off the ceiling. That feels like hours ago, but when I look at the large clock on the wall, I realize that it has only been forty- five minutes. Wow, time really flies when you're terrified out of your mind, getting swatted by a giant, and having a bunch of demonic dogs trying to rip you apart.

With everything back to normal, this means that the massive cage holding everyone is now gone and all the people who had come to watch the game are now standing on the basketball court, looking around in amazement at the fixed gym. When several peoples' eyes land on Kal though, their amazement is instantly replaced by fury and hatred. They start yelling curses at him and everyone else starts joining in. All of the people start walking closer to Kal in a crowd, demanding in angry voices for him to explain himself. Kal tries backing away from them, but soon runs out of room and bumps into a wall, leaving him without a way to escape. I hear someone shout out that he needs to be punished for what he did, and I know that with everyone angry like they are now, then they might agree with that person and end up doing something terrible that can't be fixed. I fly over the crowd and land right in front of Kal. I open my wings wide, shielding Kal from the angry mob.

"You will not hurt him!" Everyone backs away at the sound of the harsh tone in my voice. I glare at them all, letting the tension rise in my silence as they all wait to see what I plan on doing. "He had a moment of temptation with the Crow because everyone treated him poorly. Can you blame him

for that?!" Nobody looks at me, many have their eyes directed at their feet, suddenly realizing that they were going to hurt a person who has always been the victim. "Are you really going to harm someone who gave up a chance for revenge on everyone who has ever been cruel to him? He showed mercy on you, now you need to show mercy on him!" Everyone falls silent at my words, thinking about what I have said. At least everyone except one.

"Why should we?!" A familiar voice shouts out. Alex pushes his way to the front of the crowd so that he is standing in front of me. "Who knows what that freak could have done to us when the Crow was helping him!" I step forward until Alex and I are almost nose to nose. He stares down at me with a little bit of fear flashing in his eyes. He was completely confident just a second ago, but now that I, as Silver Dove, am confronting him, that confidence is long gone.

"You should because he didn't do it. He had a chance to get what he wanted but sacrificed that so that everyone would be safe. Nobody was hurt, were they?"

"Nobody was hurt! Are you kidding?! Have you completely forgotten about me?!" Everyone looks up to see that Angela is still stuck in the basketball hoop. I cover my mouth with my hand, trying to hold back the laughter. Not everybody can control themselves though, practically everyone in the crowd bursts out in giggles and laughter as I fly up to help lift her out of the hoop. Angela's face is a burning red in her embarrassment as I set her back

on the ground. She marches out of the room in a huff with the laughter following behind her as she slams the gym door. Now that a lot of the tension has disappeared after that good laugh, I turn back to the crowd with a smile.

"Now, I believe you guys were about to play a basketball game, maybe it's time for that to get started." The crowd bursts into cheers as they all start heading back to their seats on the newly fixed bleachers and the two basketball teams rush onto the court, waving their arms up and yelling at the audience to cheer louder just like they were doing before the Giant interrupted. I watch them all for a moment before I realize there is one person who doesn't have a place yet. Kal is still standing in the same spot, watching everyone awkwardly, unsure of what to do.

I smile at him as I hold out my hand. Kal slowly and cautiously takes my hand, as if he was expecting me to do something mean to him as a prank. Leading him to an empty seat in the bleachers, he sits down beside a family, made up of a dad and his two daughters. The father looks at him with uncertainty for a moment before he gives Kal a smile and a nod, clearly indicating that he is welcome to sit by them. Kal's face immediately breaks into a huge grin as he sits beside them. The youngest daughter, who looks like she is only five years old, doesn't waste a second and starts asking Kal all sorts of questions about being possessed by the Crow and what it felt like to be "so huge". Her dad tries to tell her to stop asking questions like that since he could obviously see how embarrassed Kal was, but Kal told him that it was alright and answered the little girl's questions with a patient smile. Knowing that Kal will be alright, I open my wings and take off in the air, sweeping over the basketball court as the entire crowd cheers for me and I fly straight through the gym doors and into the hallway. I sweep through a few halls until I am absolutely sure that I am alone. Only then do I land and let myself transform back into my usual self.

I hurry off to get back to the gym so I can watch the game. When I get there, I cautiously look inside, making sure that nobody will spot me sneaking in, but nobody is paying any attention to me, they are too busy watching the game. I walk in and sit down on the first empty seat I find and turn my attention to the game. Alex shoots a basket and makes it in easily, earning our school's team a few points. He glances into the audience and notices me. Alex gives me a wave and a charming wink. A few girls sitting nearby me practically faint with delight, all of them telling each other that that wink was meant for them. I know that they want that wink to be for them, but I know its for me, but I wish I could give it to them since I surely don't want it. The other girls in school can fawn all over that guy, but I'm not going to fall for his cheap tricks.

I don't pay attention to him, instead my eyes are scanning the crowd, looking for someone else. My heart seems to beat faster as fear rushes through me. Where is Luis? I know that he should be safe since I used my medal to make everything go back to normal, but where is he? I haven't seen him since the bake sale meeting before the game. My heart pounds furiously in my chest when another sudden thought rushes through my mind. I haven't seen him since the Crow showed up. Does Luis know something? Was he involved?

I shake my head softly, trying to get rid of those thoughts. I have thought that Luis was the Crow before and I was proven wrong, I can't just start thinking it's him again, that wouldn't make any sense. I need to be calm and think this through, there are probably other explanations for why he isn't here. I'm just being crazy by jumping to conclusions like this. I try to pay attention to the game and a lot of time passes, but the problem is that even though time has passed, Luis still isn't here. The game is almost over, but he is still missing. This only makes the dark thought keep swirling in my mind; is Luis involved with the Crow?

Chapter Eighteen
Luis-
After the
Game

I've been wandering through the hallways without any idea of where I'm going. I just feel like I need to clear my head and be alone. My mind keeps going back to everything that happened with the Giant and Silver Dove, but mostly I think about how I acted with them. What on earth was I doing? Why was I acting like that? When I had transformed the others before, I never really did anything bad to them, but I hit the Giant multiple times, slapping him in the face with my wings and threatening him. Why did I do that? Why was I acting like that to a nice guy like Kal? Silver Dove even pointed that out to him, that I was not being good to him.

My footsteps echo in the empty hallway, making me feel even lonelier than I already do. I can feel my stomach churning and my heart sinking into my chest as I realize the truth. I was being worse to Kal than his bullies were before I transformed him. His bullies were only hurting him with words, I was hurting him with words and violence. I was worse than the bullies, I was worse than the people I am trying to fight against.

I punch one of the lockers in my rage and I instantly regret it when a wave of pain rushes through my hand and down my arm. I shake my hand to try and get rid of the pain. Yeah, that was stupid, that was really stupid. Once the pain has disappeared, I put my hands in my pockets and continue walking down the hall with my head lowered. What has happened to me? Why did I act so differently this time? I shake my head, disappointed in myself. It doesn't matter why I did it, I did it, that's what matters.

My mind wanders back to when I first started my mission as the Crow. I had such high hopes then, I thought I was going to be the good guy, and I was going to make things better for everyone. When I think back on what I did tonight though I can't help but wonder, did I make anything better for anybody? Have a made things better at all during my entire time as the Crow?

I hear my footsteps echoing down the hall as my mind remembers all of the people I have transformed, how they were at the time I transformed them and how they are now. Jade Elizabeth has become a bit more confident now since she was transformed into Tigerclaw. Cheyanne now hangs out with better friends than before I transformed her into the Sprinter. Rosie now runs her own gardening club and has some friends because of that. And I've heard that Shay is a lot happier since the day last summer I transformed her into the Beauty Queen. My heavy heart suddenly feels a little bit lighter, maybe I have done some good as the Crow. I let this thought sink in for a few minutes as my steps no longer drag across the floor as I pass through the halls. I'm right, I have done some good. This isn't a battle that I need to give up on yet. Maybe Kal will change too and he will be happier after his experience with me too, I just need to sit back and wait.

Heading back to the gym, I walk through the doors to see that the game is almost over. I don't really care about this since I couldn't care less about sports, so I just search the crowd for Colomba. My eyes spot her almost immediately, she always stands out in a crowd to me, like a diamond in pile of rocks. As soon as she spots me, she smiles at me and waves at me to come over and sit with her. I eagerly follow her instructions.

Neither of us say a word to each other as I sit down beside her, we just exchange a smile as we turn our attention to watch the last minutes of the game tick down on the clock and the players run around the court, trying to do something, I have no idea what though. I never learned the rules of this game, sports will never be my thing. As Alex gets the ball into the hoop thing, the crowd cheers, but I don't think Colomba really cares about this game either since she turns to me to ask me a question.

"Hey Luis where have you been?" My heart leaps in my chest at her question, but I instantly calm down when I realize that she isn't asking for any bad reason like she's suspicious of me, she has probably just been worried about me since I went missing during everything that happened between me and Silver Dove. I smile at her, trying to get rid of her worries.

"Oh, I had been in the bathroom in the hallway when the Crow showed up, so I was cornered in there by his shadow dogs. After he disappeared, I took a walk around the school trying to calm down a bit since I had been pretty shaken up." Colomba smiles at me, believing what I have told her, before she turns her attention back to the game.

Our team is down by two points with only seconds to go. Alex has the ball right now. It doesn't surprise me at all that Alex makes the winning point and everyone cheers for him. The entire team lifts him up and starts carrying him on their shoulders. The home team's crowd runs onto the court to join the celebration, but Colomba and I stay behind. We just watch as everyone else cheers. Even though we don't say it out loud, I think we both feel the same way, we don't want to cheer for him, not for Alex.

The two of us head out into the entryway of the school so that we can get to the bake sale table before the crowd leaves the gym. It's our turn to man the table. Kal comes to join us only a moment later, looking at us with a bit of embarrassment on his face. He obviously feels a bit awkward being around us when about an hour or so ago he was trashing the gym. Colomba and I both give him a smile and he can obviously see that he is welcome with the two of us. As the three of us prepare everything for the sudden rush of people to leave the gym, I have a sudden urge to go over and apologize to him for what happened. I quickly get that out of my head though. I can't just apologize to him, he would be so confused at first, but then he might figure out what I mean and might realize that I am the Crow. I can't risk doing something that stupid.

The crowd leaves the gym and a ton of people surround our table as they try to buy everything left of the baked goods. I'm not surprised that by the end of the night, all of Colomba's cupcakes are gone while there is only one little bag left of my dulce de coco. As soon as the crowd is gone, when Colomba sees that there is just one bag left, she pulls out her purse and takes out a dollar to buy it. When the dollar is placed in the little metal box of money, she pulls one out of the little bag and takes a bite, smiling at the sweet taste. She compliments me on them, and I can feel myself blush as I thank her. All the people who were helping with the bake sale clean everything up before heading home. Colomba and I both get in my uncle's car and he takes Colomba home before we return to our little apartment above his antique shop.

As soon as I've walked through the door, I head to my room, completely exhausted after everything that has happened tonight. I take off my shoes and toss them in my closet before I go over to my dresser and pull out my sketchpad, my special sketchpad. Within the pages of this, I have my own kind of record of my time as the Crow. I have drawn all of the soldiers I've had in the past, and today I will be adding another one. Pulling out a pencil, I flop down on my bed and start sketching.

While my pencil is slowly making its way

across the page, I think about everything that happened tonight. When Silver Dove grabbed me like that, for a second, I thought she was going to kill me. When I looked past her mask and into those eyes, I could see so much hatred that I wouldn't have been surprised if she did kill me. With her super strength, she wouldn't have any difficulty with doing that. Within the span of a few seconds, I think of a dozen ways that she could have killed me with her amazing strength. I have to stop drawing for a moment as a shudder passes through me at the thought. I let my mind go blank as I finish up my drawing. When it is complete, I hold it up to the light so that I can examine it more properly. I smile at the result.

I drew the Giant standing over the school. He is looking down at it with an evil smile that just screams to the world that he has terrible things planned for the school. Too bad the real Giant didn't do the terrible things I was hoping he would do. I slam my sketchbook shut as I glare out my window. This is the seventh time that I've failed against Silver Dove. What am I doing wrong? Why do I keep failing with this? I give these people amazing powers so they can get what they want and then they just give them up after Silver Dove talks to them? What's up with that? Why are they always changing their minds when they were so dead set on getting revenge right before she showed up? It doesn't make any sense.

When I think about all the things that people have done to me, I want revenge more than anything. I want all of those people to feel the pain I felt. Maybe once they feel that pain they will understand. Maybe then they can treat others with respect. The way they should treat me with respect.

I can only hope that Kal will be okay though. He is a nice guy, and he deserves better treatment than the way everyone has been treating him. Just like me, he deserves respect. My eyes glare out the window as the stars stare back down at me. The night looks almost cheerful, with the moon shining brightly above me like a silver spotlight in the sky. The cheerfulness of the night feels like it's mocking me. I lower the blinds at my window, blocking it from view. Even though it is still a bit early for it, I get ready for bed and get under the covers. I want to go to bed now so that this day will be over faster, and a new day can begin. Hopefully, tomorrow won't be so disappointing.

Chapter Nineteen
Colomba-
The Next
Day

As I pass through the front doors of the school, the hallway is already buzzing with excitement even though it is still early in the morning. Everyone is talking about what happened at the game last night. Nobody is really interested about how our team won, they are just talking about what happened with Kal when he was the Giant. All of the people who weren't there are listening excitedly to the people who were as they tell them every detail about what went down. I have to keep myself from laughing when I hear several people exaggerating about things that happened. One person even said that I had beaten up the Crow and almost killed him, that one I did not laugh at, it made me feel sick to my stomach. Did they really think I could hurt somebody like that? What was I to them, a monster? They really must think that since all the people listening to that story seem to believe every word and nobody defends me.

Nobody stands up to the person telling the story and tells them that Silver Dove would not do that. Nobody cares.

Am I just somebody for everyone to gossip and spread rumors about? While the person tells the story, still talking about how vicious I was, the people around them absorb every detail while the story teller seems to glow under all of their attention. As I watch the story teller's smug face smile as someone asks them if Silver Dove really punched the Crow's face so hard that his mask almost shattered, I have the strong urge to just punch them in the face. I want to shatter that smile and scream at them for spreading such hurtful lies about me, convincing all of these people around them that I'm some kind of demon.

I keep walking though, I can't let their words break me. No matter what they say, I have to stay strong. If I strike out at these people like I really want to, then I will be the monster they are making me out to be. I can't let them win. My feet carry me past them, but my mind remains with them. In my head, I keep hearing them repeating over and over the hurtful things they were saying about me, all of their lies. Their words still echo in my head as I make it to my first class and I sit at my desk. As my head starts to ache listening to the harsh words in my mind, I realize that this is going to be a very long day.

Most of the day creeped past me at a snail's pace. By the time lunch rolled around, I was ready to hit my head against the wall I was so frustrated. In every class I went to, whenever I was walking down the hall, it seemed that there was a new rumor being spread about what happened last night. Now the day is almost over, and I am so grateful for that. For a while there, I thought that today was never going to end.

The final bell will be ringing soon and then I can finally leave. I am walking down the hall, heading back to class from the library when I see a familiar face ahead of me. I run up to greet them, but I stop for a moment when I realize that they may not want to talk to me. After everything that happened last night, they may not want to talk to anybody. When I watch them continue walking away from me though, I can't help myself, and I run up to them again.

"Hello Kal." He jumps a little in surprise at my sudden arrival before he gives me an awkward smile.

"Hey Colomba, how's it going?" I smile warmly at him, hoping that this can make him feel more comfortable with me and he won't feel so awkward.

"Going good." I look at the shirt he's wearing to see that it is one of the shirts that the track team wears. "Did you join the track team?" He blushes a little as he looks away from me.

"Well, not exactly. I'm too out of shape for that. After what happened with the Crow, and, you know, everything before that, I am really going to try and lose weight. I don't want to do this to be accepted anymore, I just want to be healthier. I told the track coach this and they told me that I can join in their training so that I can get better and maybe one day I can actually join the team. That one senior, Cheyanne, who got transformed by the Crow last year, is even going to help me. She is so nice. Hopefully we can work hard enough that I can reach my goal." I smile at him, feeling so proud.

"Judging from how determined you sound, I'm guessing that you will reach that goal." He smiles as he lowers his head to try and hide his blushing cheeks, a little embarrassed by my compliment.

"Thanks, look I'm sorry about what happened the other day at the bake sale thing. You were just trying to be nice to me and I snapped at you. I didn't want to be mean by that, I was just upset. I-" I interrupt him, placing my hand on his large shoulder to comfort him, knowing that it is hurting his pride to say all these things.

"It's okay, I understand. They were being cruel to you and you lashed out. It's normal. Hopefully you won't have to deal with that anymore." The final bell interrupts us and all the other students start piling out of the classrooms, everyone eager to get home. I smile up at Kal. "It was great seeing you again, and I hope you do well with your goals. You deserve it." He smiles back at me and the two of us walk away, not another word was needed to be said.

I enter the crowd of students heading to the front doors. The noise coming from all the students in the hall is a dull roar of feet shuffling, laughter, and people talking excitedly about what they plan on doing this weekend. A sigh of relief leaves me as I see the front doors of the school. Soon I will be on the bus with Nat and Luis and we can talk and laugh, then I can go home and today will be over. Maybe on Monday when we get back to school everything will be back to normal. Maybe then all the rumors about Silver Dove will be gone. Maybe then I can come to school without having to worry about this and I can be happy again. This little hope of mine does not last long though, it, of course, has to be ruined.

When I pass through the doors, I overhear someone talking about a girl from my English class, and they aren't saying very kind things about her either. The girl who is saying these terrible things is giggling about it to a group of friends, and they all agree with her even though I know for sure that what they are saying is not true. Within the moving crowd, I stand still, completely stunned by what I am witnessing.

Just last night, I was defending someone as Silver Dove, trying to convince these people to stop hurting Kal, to stop hurting everyone, so that they won't feel as if they have to join sides with the Crow. Even though I said this just last night, someone is already spreading more rumors and lies about someone else and nobody is trying to stop them. Am I doing all of this, risking so much, for nothing? Are any of these people going to change?

The Crow has transformed six people in this school already because of all the bullying going on here, but the problem is still here? Why aren't they learning their lesson? Why are they so blind? Can't they see that this is just going to make the Crow come back again? Am I the only one seeing sense in this school?

A menacing cloud suddenly comes over me as a dark thought races through my mind. I'm not the only one seeing sense, the Crow is seeing it too, that's why he has been doing all of this. The dark cloud seems to grow heavier and heavier over me as another thought invades my mind. Is he right? Am I really on the bad guy's side? Am I really just letting these people get away with how they treat others because I keep saving them? What if I didn't save them the next time the Crow shows up again? What if I let him win at least once? Would they get the picture then? Would they treat each other better after that?

I hang my head as I start walking to the bus again, my soul feeling as if it is dragging across the ground as I walk. I feel so lost, unsure if I am the hero or the villain.

Don't miss the previous books in The Adventures of Silver Dove series.

Eliza Scalia is a therapist who has a master's degree in Clinical Mental Health from Troy University. She enjoys reading, writing, and needlework, as well as hanging out with her pet cat, Dusty. Eliza has been writing since she was in middle school and has self- published the Death's Assistant series for young adults.